I0676725

MICHAEL GARDNER'S

American in a Sense: City in a Garden

ISBN Number: 978 - 0 – 615 - 26647- 3
Library of Congress Control Number: 2008911212

Michael Gardner for New Age Scribes Publishing, Inc

Cover Designed by Lafayette K. Ford for Koldkreations Graphiks
Contact: koldkreation@gmail.com

Keys

The truth of America is that with the exception of the original natives, everyone here is from someplace else. Some were deemed immigrants and others imported goods or servants. Either way, none were invited to come over by the native environment and thus can be termed as invaders. What if nature only provided enough resources for the survival of the original inhabitants? Then, these invaders are here and must organize for the survival of all or for only the strong. But who are the strong? Because amongst these invaders are sub-cultures which separate the invading human beings into a society of many groups and cultures. From the arrival of these invaders came a mathematic problem; since we are here, how can we survive together without killing each other? Many philosophers attempted to prescribe an answer to this problem. I provide you with their quotes as keys to aid you in the intent of this work.

Social order was thus a human creation designed to end the war of every man against every man-
Hobbes

A man of thorough good breeding that is, one with proper liberal education and virtue, is incapable of doing a rude and brutal action and thus does not require the threat of punishment-
Shaftsbury

Yet this book deals with the heart of America which we call urban, or the streets. The best ideal to define the reasoning behind the secret societies of the street is stated by John Locke in his social contract theory (which was also a major influence on our U.S. constitution). This theory states

if everything in this world is created by God, then God is in control of everything and sets laws for everything before it was created. With this in mind, the state of nature has the law of nature to govern it, which obliges everyone. And Reason, which is that law, teaches all of mankind who will but consult it that, being all equal and independent, that no one will harm another in his life, health, liberty, or possessions. If everything belongs to everyone, then everyone can take everything including someone else's life, then we must bind together in a social contract for the survival of mankind.

So be it in America and all of its communities.

Acknowledgements

This work acknowledges all of humanity and its spirit of fraternal support. In witnessing the good works of what humanity has done throughout history the author has been inspired to further the development of the relationships of all people that connect with each other to uplift others like themselves regardless of differences. The author would also like to acknowledge the American People as a society of leaders that are developing beyond the great barriers that were created by misled thoughts of the past. We now share a President of a descent that was once seen as beneath human in which the American people as one unit has chosen. Along with that the author acknowledges the many communities & cultures of the United States of America that are coming together to express power of change against an old system. The author recognizes Chicago as one of the most segregated cities of the world & its effort to change its condition through the works of its people.

Dedication

Last but not least the author would like to dedicate this book to the under privileged that are last to experience the American fraternal love as a people & would like to extend hope to them as the future holds a more equal America. Included in this dedication are Chicago Projects with emphasis on Henry Horner Homes with emphasis on 2215, 2245, 2145, 2111, 124, & 2051 as the influence of this work. (**Rest in peace Seneca "Skip' Wright, Corey 'Silky C' Harris, Joseph 'GD' Logan, & Byron 'Big B' Logan and over 500 other Chicago youth that passed from violence but are not forgotten by beloved friends & family).** Cabrini Green, Rockwell Gardens, Harold Ickes, Stateway Gardens, and all project housing developments have created beings that are able to overcome the greatest struggles of the world. Those to whom the author could not have completed this work without their support include the Gardner family including Brandi McGhee and my three beloved children, Chicago's 'Street Organizations,' Freemasonry, Kappa Alpha Psi Fraternity, Inc. with emphasis on its 'Hard Hitting' Harvey- Markham Alumni Chapter, Terrell McCullough, Lafayette Kyle Ford, Basil Muhammad, Dorian Cleary, & many other supportive friends that never gave up on me & supported the crystallization of a dream. Chicago this work is your voice!

Introduction

Someone once said that America does not want reality, America wants entertainment- Unknown

You have just opened up a door through time when you spread the pages of this book. Now quickly, put on this fireproof suit so that you can be safe. It's the year 2019. My city is on fire again. We the inhabitants are choking and dying away in droves due to the smoke of despair hanging over our heads. It's hot! I see people running in fear, to the point where they will not even stop to help each other. Panic is how we live in these days, as the only thing that is being offered to quell this fire is more bodies and more blood. The thing is that we can actually put out this great fire if we all just come together. What happened, you ask? Well, hop into my machine with me to keep safe from this inferno as I begin to take you through the events that lead to this fire. This city has endured its share of fires: one in 1871 in which only our water tower was left standing; one in 1920 that started at a Southside beach and burned through our city for weeks until there was so much blood spilled they termed the time period the Red Summer--it was sooo hot! The other was in 2008, where the fire soared so high that even those in the downtown buildings were not safe as the city's annual event the Taste of Chicago witnessed lives taken by the fire. The resources needed to prepare us all to prevent this fire from taking the lives of citizens again were not being offered to us equally, and so when some of us thought they would survive without all of us, we fell into the same situation again.

American in a Sense is a time machine that takes you on a ride through the development of the social conscience of America. The scene of this book is set in one of the largest cities in the world, whose violence has grown to dominate headlines around the world. This city was built by all races across the globe and is said to be the most segregated of all cities. This piece does not steer away from the things that certain cultures do to adapt to an environment. It does not steer away from the fact that in the human condition, many will take lives to survive. This book goes right through the murder and mayhem that people do to survive. The book also goes through the bonds that were formed in the interest of cultural survival in America. This book also brings up positive methods that many American cultures use to survive. The past is the key to the future-- will history repeat itself? The end result is directed at a self-healing process. The intent of this book is for America to reflect and diagnose itself. Can this city thrive as an example of a unified country which we call America? The first step is admitting that there is a problem--an American problem!

Prologue

I have found you. You have been hiding from me for years, out of fear of facing me. You can't escape me, for I dwell within the depths of your mind. You hear me when I talk to you every day and choose to listen sometimes, but most of the time you ignore me. Oh, you don't remember me now? I developed with you in the womb. You use me to balance your life, but when credit is due to me, I'm looked over. Who am I? I am *Reason* and I dwell within your inner consciousness.

Don't listen to that voice! I am your strength; I give you power beyond measure. When you are attacked and backed into a corner, it is I that fight your way out. I have always been here but only show myself when needed most. I remind you to eat food and drink water each day! I remind you to wake up, to keep going, to breathe, to survive! I am *Instinct*.

Reason versus *Instinct* in a developing nation called America--just watching the battle is most entertaining. Who will win?

Open me.

1

True story…

Kids returning home happily and hastily from school past tall sky-scraping buildings near downtown to enter into one of those buildings which they called home. A teen named Sconey was sitting at the corner door of one of the buildings facing one of the other large 22-story buildings. The building looked like a fort made of red brick as a shadow seemed to loom over it. Sconey had been having a gut-wrenching feeling that something bad was going to happen this day.

Sconey tells Michael, whom they call Mike or MG, "You know I feel kind of sick. Aye, go watch Satin, I think somethin's gonna happen."

Mike (MG), having the same kind of feeling, says, "I think so, too."

He walks down the concrete pavement and corridor, past the two steel elevators and the security guard gate, which no security guard has appeared for weeks, to the long corridor entry way, to the visibility of little kids coming through the second steel door of the first of the main entryway corridors. There was the noise of laughter, cheer, and the pitter-patter of little feet coming in. Satin is at the front of the building, looking out and scouting the enemy to approach, constantly, constantly. MG was on his way to the front to look for Satin and asked, "Where's my gun?" I'm a go out to this front and watch Satin's back. I need my gun."

MG was known to have two guns on him at a time but this day could find neither. He was a keeper of guns, but this day he didn't have a gun on him; they were passed out before he got there, and he left his trusty guns, *Thunder* and *Lighting*, upstairs, as he was just on a small trip just to see what could be going on downstairs, as he often did. MG was like the caretaker of all the youth. Being a youth himself he just seemed to be more altruistic. MG didn't really stay in the building; he just came because he wanted to look out for his guys, and of course it was his place of employment. I mean, at least, not on the legal radar, but on the scene of the streets. So, as MG stopped by the station of the third door stronghold, which was closer to the main entrance--but not close enough, as there was a long corridor between the two--he stopped to ask, "Do any of you have any extra guns?"

T and Hawk answered, "Uh unh."

MG went to the front corridor anyway, then, with the gut-wrenching feeling increasing, and saw Satin there. Mike was convinced that Satin had a gun; he always had a gun. MG approached and passed the kids to make sure Satin was all right, by tapping him on the shoulder. Satin turned for a second and spoke to MG and said, "Everything's good here."

But he never said if he had the gun or not, and MG was not sure. MG turned and had this feeling, so he was not going to take it anymore. MG's thoughts were to go upstairs and get his trusty guns just in case, and within seconds he only made just an acute turn of his head, away from Satin, when one of the kids all of sudden had a growth spurt and got tall. This child's hair was donned with the dress of a black hooded sweater and curly locks with an unseen face. As this child rose, the darkness of the corridors turned to light. Sounds and time seemed to stand still as they saw flash, flash, flash, flash, flash. Kids scattered. MG, not knowing his motion, feeling time move in a way in which the amount of seconds seemed like an eternity, turned back real close to Satin to see what exactly was going on with Satin, these flashes, and himself. But it seemed to be over as MG and Satin lay on the ground, just past the second set of steel doors that were able to lock anyone in or out. All the children seemed to be gone, all extra people except the members of the organization seemed to have disappeared, not to be seen anywhere around. MG takes his breath slowly, *Huhhhh....huhhh*. He finally looks around as time seems to be returning to its regular schedule. Sound seems to be turning back into its regular pace. And the first sounds into MG's ears were not the sounds of joy, but those of pain. He looks to see where the sound is coming from and he hears laughter coming from Satin.

MG gets up and says, "Satin, you... you cool?"

As Satin laughs, his laughter begins to stop and turns into a scream of "Ohhhhh, they got me, them muthafucka's got me, but I'm aight."

MG looks. He can't see any blood but if Satin says he's hit, then he's hit. The first thought through MG's mind is, *I'm right by him.* MG checks himself.

Right in the vicinity of MG, in the line of fire, was Gino, Hawk and T. As they all turned to look at each other and search each other, they're fine, all through the line of fire. Only one down is Satin, who's screaming. A crowd starts to gather to see what's happening, only after prior knowledge that the police and ambulance were underway and that it was safe to come out. MG looks up to see the Black hooded figure that once looked like a child fleeing and fading fast into the distance.

It was a man--damn, they got us!

The guys of 2215 looked at each other, as they were coming out of a daze, with the thought on their mind that a hit was just completed. That their lives could have been stopped just seconds ago. A feeling of sadness overtook all of the guys of 2215 as they looked upon Satin and knew that that could have been any one of them. Yet MG, being the caretaker and most altruistic of them, thought, *Why was it Satin? He is only 14. Why did anyone have to get hit?* There were so many traumatic thoughts going through MG's mind about what just happened such as how Satin, a 14 year old, was shot; the feeling of sadness for his family; the fact that he almost lost his own life and much more...

MG's compassion immediately turned to rage as he shouted towards the other teens, "Where the fuck were my guns when I needed them! Why didn't anyone else have a gun on them! It's fucking war out here!"

The crowd around is mixed with emotions of sympathy, anger, and panic at the plight of the 14 year old Satin. Satin's family came downstairs after hearing what happened. The crowd was telling Satin, lying on the ground, that everything was going to be okay, the ambulance is on its way.

All Satin was saying is what any young "soldier" in the neighborhood would say to the public, "They got me, they got me, man, them muthafuckas got me." He said this repeatedly. "It's okay though, I'll be back at em'--imma' live."

13

Then he lets out a scream louder than the first one, "OOOOOOhhhhhh!!!!!"

But he tries to control how he is yelling to cater to male pride of how young soldiers adapt to such an environment. MG looked at him as if he was taking it like a man, as they say. But MG thought, *How can you be a man at 14?* MG felt what was coming before it even happened and was powerless to do much about it.

As the paramedics carried Satin to the ambulance he shouted out, "I'll be back, motherfuckers, just watch, y'all motherfuckers is dead!"

Satin never made it back from the hospital to exact his revenge on his killers. When the Crime Scene investigators entered the area, they wasted no time in gathering evidence and getting informants to give any information. They came and left quickly, calling it a day.

The investigation was not thorough, as the investigators were rumored to be part of a cover-up. A licensed clinical social worker came on the scene to soothe the youth's family, along with the community. The community was more trusting of the worker than the police and opened up all information to her, information that led her to believe that the cover-up was true. The social worker asked what people might Satin or his organization have worked with that could have wanted him and his other members dead.

Many of the community had their eyes wide and their voices lowered as if their lives were in danger as they answered with the names of those connected. Such powerful people were involved that the worker couldn't report them to her boss or agency. These people were her agency's financial backers and bosses. She would need someone she could trust to help herself and that community. She frantically raised her brick-sized cellular phone to place a call to a friend of hers from college that worked in the higher levels of law enforcement.

Ring, ring, riiinnngggg, goes a phone in a distant place.

"Federal Bureau of Investigations, Agent Khan Chi speaking."

Welcome to the past that will take you into the future and beyond. The first question at hand that would link the future to the present is in the past--who was the killer? America likes a gangster story, and finding this killer will take you on a ride through the world's greatest gangster murder thriller ever.

2

Find the killer

Ring-Ring- Ring.

"Hello," man on the other end of the phone answers.

The man on the phone is looking out his office window upon a city that he is king of. He is the mayor. He is an Irishman of a "regular" height with a tailor-made suit. His office is equipped with a large, wine-colored leather chair that resembles a king's throne in an office setting. He often looks at his city from a large window in his Downtown office in the penthouse office of a 60-story skyscraper. He has shoulders that are square with the confidence of being the head man of the world's second most powerful city, the city that works, Chicago. To be the mayor of this city is equivalent to being the President of the U.S. Chicago isn't a city it's a nation in the minds of its residents. Dick heads that nation and has for years. He is untouchable. He is way too busy to answer a phone but it's on his red line, so it must be important. As Dick repeats hello again, the voice of his assistant begins to speak, panicking,

"Sir the F-B—"

The large doors swing open as a dark-haired, dark-eyed, tall man walks furiously in Dick's direction. There are other men and women behind him. Dick looks puzzled, as no one dares to barge into the door of the Mayor of the world's second city unless, it's the –

"FBI!" the men said. "We need you to come with us for questioning."

Dick retorts, "Where is my security?" as CPD officers come in right behind the Federal agents, with their guns out. Dick yells to them with the voice of strong authority, "Do you know who I am?"

The Fed in charge responds to him, "Do you know who *I* am?"

Dick sits in his large, throne-like chair as he recalls the face of the most notorious FBI agent in America since the fabled Untouchable's Elliot Ness. He went by the name of Khan. He made a name for himself as the arresting officer of corrupt politicians, law enforcement officials, and high-end criminals everywhere. He was feared, as he had been known to take down the most powerful politicians and bureaucratic leaders of America. Dick's cockiness would not subside as he looked at his CPD as they held their weapons high in the faces of the famed FBI.

Dick asked, as he is still boss, "What do you want with me? I got a city to run."

Khan answered him, "You are wanted for questioning, and your officers need to lower their weapons before there is a mess in here!"

"You came into my office--"

"I'm not asking. Lower your weapons!"

"On what charge am I being questioned?" screamed Dick.

"There is no more talking," said Khan, as the FBI agents felt the heat of the room and moisture form around their index fingers that were itching to a gravitational pull of the .45 caliber automatics that they held. Their arms were held with elbows locked in perfect angles that extended into solidly formed hands and piercing eyes on targets, waiting on the sound or word of what to do next.

"Stand down!" yelled Dick. "Now, why did you say you came here to waste this good city's time again? I've beat your patronage charges-- what else do you want me for?" he added, with a smug, conceited look on his face.

"Murder," Khan said with authority.

"What?!"

Khan repeated, "The murder of a fourteen year old in Horner."

The semi-smile on Dick's face began to sink into a look of awe as Khan reached for his arm. The surrounding officers were stunned to hear the news.

A phone went off in the hand of a man surrounded by body guards bearing arms and with the faces of the most serious of soldiers.

When the smoke clears

3

A Black man called Chief picks up his cell phone as he walks, surrounded by four huge men dressed in Black, as if they were body guards. The man is walking the streets of Chicago's notorious Englewood neighborhood. The other younger men in the neighborhood seem to be on alert and looking out for anything to happen. There seem to be an abundance of men, from teens to the mid-30s, out in the neighborhood today.

"Chief! Whaddup?" One of the youth signals to him.

The man on the cell phone seems to command a lot of respect from those in the neighborhood. He is in a pin-striped suit with dark sunglasses that look expensive--very different from the youth and others around who don the latest fashion of the streets like jogging suits and gold chains. The best sneakers money can buy, that was their style, but him he was of another caliber. The cars around were painted with the most fluorescent colors and their tires bore the shiniest chrome shoes. The man called

Chief was being escorted to his black Yukon with tinted windows, as if he were the president of the U.S. walking to his motorcade, when he answered the phone again. "Speak- who this?"

"G-five-o, nightshade," the voice said. "They've been watching us all day!"

Chief threw up a hand gesture and there seemed to be a lot of whistling from one corner to the next. The surrounding men moved like soldiers into a defensive position as a black Impala raced up the street in the direction of Chief. The entire scene changed as the children playing in the surrounding streets disappeared. There were bikes still rolling around with no riders; basketballs bounced their last movements as they began to roll; there was the bang as the last door of an elderly citizen slammed after she was finally able to get in the house. Out of nowhere came a Caprice and then a navy blue Excursion from the wrong direction of a one-way street. Lights were flashing red, white, and blue and men and women were yelling, "FBI!"

Uniformed men and women in vests came running from all directions. Some of them were dressed in jogging suits, as if under cover. One would think that the game was over for Chief and his body guards, but then, you couldn't see the rest of the picture. There were guys on the roof tops in white tee shirts with automatic weapons, there were boxy Chevy Caprices pulling up with guns blazing, men were jumping out while the cars were still moving. It looked like the modern version of a cowboy showdown. Chief moves his phone to his pocket as a man with dark hair and dark eyes slowly approaches.

"Agent Khan, your men need to be smarter," said Chief.

"Call your dogs off, Chief or shall I say Lawence Malik alias known as Chief G Law, we don't need any bloodshed. I just want to ask you some questions."

"First of all stop calling out m government name! Secondly, you doing all this for me? Is it my birthday? Y'all pull up on me in my neighborhood. My streets like y'all, my family. I didn't hear nobody yellin' surprise!" Chief was smiling as his 400-pound body guard held his tech nine in Khan's direction.

"Lawrence, I got 30 trained agents ready to take a life if they have to. What--you got 40 men, or shall I say 25 children and 15 adults? Are you willing to sacrifice them?"

"I don't know; let me ask them if they ready to sacrifice me," Chief laughed. "What y'all say people and folks?"

Chief's soldiers replied, "Man, fuck the police!"

Khan laughed and shouted out, "Can't y'all spell? Look, let me help you--three letters--F-B-I."

Chief told his guards to put their guns away as he slowly approached Khan. "I got this; he ain't no threat."

Chief whispered into Khan's ear, "Look, Khan, let my guys get out of here and we ain't got no beef. I'll go with you."

" Stand down!" ordered Khan.

"But sir!" protested an agent.

"That's an order, damnit!"

The agents hesitantly placed their weapons in their cars and holsters; so did the surrounding youth.

Chief yelled out to his guys, "If you don't want yo' ass in jail for ten plus years or to be violated, get the fuck up outta here in five minutes."

As cars screeched and windows closed, there was nothing left but the sounds of pitter-patter. All one could hear were the sounds of loud music playing in the distance as one of the cars sped away. "Ain't nothing but a G thang, Baby- them low-down G's gone crazy" became distant words.

All you could see was smoke and dust as Chief walked into the Excursion with a couple of agents. As the smoke cleared, Chief asked "By the way, Khan, what am I being questioned for?"

"Murder."

The phone rings, and a man on the other end, sitting in his corporate office in the local 750 labor union office on Chicago's near Westside, picks up.

Corporate Dealings

4

"Mr. Giancana speaking."

"This is Charlene," his lawyer speaks to him with anxiety in her voice. "You don't have much time; the FBI should be there any second. I will meet you at their headquarters. You are being charged with murder."

"Really," said Giancana, as if he had no worries.

Giancana got off the phone and began to put on his tailored Italian sport coat. He only wore Italian clothing and shoes, as he took great pride in his heritage. He then lit a Cuban cigar and savored the taste that had a calming effect on him. He walked out of the office and got on the elevator. As he got off and went out of the front glass doors, the FBI agents looked astonished as he walked up to them, cocky as ever.

"Which one of you is Khan?"

Agent Khan walked up to him, not surprised that he knew they were coming. He walked up to the truck that Khan stood by as he walked toward him. Giancana walked past Khan saying, "No need for the bracelets," as he opened the door and got in. Khan was a little impressed as they sped off.

Giancana stated, "Murder, huh? You know you fucked up right? Ha-ha-ha. Can we make this quick? The wife is cooking Tuscan T-bone--my favorite!"

Khan replied, "Tell her to wrap it up and save it. You'll be eating these questions tonight and if you're guilty, maybe 25 to life."

The Inquisition

5

Dick said, "I thought you Feds believed in Miranda rights, since it was you who first forced it on the citizens? Are we going to wait for my lawyer?"

Khan replied, "Why do you need a lawyer so badly? You're only here for questions concerning the death of a fourteen year old on the West side of what you call your town. What do you have to hide that you need a lawyer to buffer?"

Dick snarled, "We both know that this is frivolous! I don't have any time to entertain this, but what do I have to do with a fourteen year old kid in the projects? I've never even paid a visit to the site."

"Your name came up during questioning and the people mentioned some interesting things about you and your past that give us enough to at least charge you with conspiracy and accessory to the murder."

"What could possibly place me in a position as an accessory or conspirator?" shouted Dick.

Khan then walked up to him as closely as possible and looked him in his eyes, his own eyes so piercing that Dick could feel him in his aura as he said, "Oh, you forgot how you started out?"

Dick sat back in his small and uncomfortable wooden chair as the scene around him began to disappear and became a new scene. The walls around him turned into a Chicago summer-blue sky. As he looked, he found himself on the baseball field that he played on as a teen, feet planted in a dirt lot in Chicago's Irish community of Bridgeport. As he swung a stick and hit a ball that came his way, all he could hear were screams from his childhood running buddies. "Run, Ritchie, run!" Ritchie woke up from the stupor and ran toward the new base mats that a local realtor bought for them.

After the game the realtor asked us if we wanted to make some money. Of course, in those days us young Irishmen could use a dollar, and this realtor kept them coming as long as we would do his bidding. He told us that there were some niggers looking to buy property near the neighborhood. We knew the drill; we had done it before. We gripped our sticks and rocks as hard as our Irish pride and walked with the stride of hell's most feared fallen angels, as only the Hamburg could do.

"There they are," Mickey screamed as our stride became a light jog and our light jog became a quick stride. Then I found the other end of my stick embedded into the head of the mother as my shirt became red with the squirt of her blood. Mickey and Larry tore into the son as the other seven threw rocks at the father, along with the other sticks and bottles that they could find. We wouldn't stop until those niggers were down or gone. The older men of the neighborhood would join us, as they wanted to ensure that the larger father of the niggers did not overpower us.

I remember the father as he ran, stumbling to jump over his wife and child to protect them. I was a little scared, as he could have easily swung to knock us out, but his only concern seemed to be his family and their protection. With respect, we kind of went light on him, so as to give him room to get outta there. We weren't animals, you know. We were just protecting what was ours. Yeah, the neighborhood stood together. Bridgeport was ours and all niggers would remember that after this, we thought. The neighborhood was a solid unit. It was us against the world. I remember my pa would tell us about the old days, days where Irish were as low on the social totem pole as the niggers, where a good Irish man had to work twice as hard as the English to make half their wages. The thing was, we stayed on the same continent with them. Yet we weren't considered as white as them until the 20th century. Now we are white, that means the world. My pa could get jobs that my gramps never dreamed of.

My pa was the owner of his own convenience store in the neighborhood. He gained respect as he took care of every family. They had credit that they sometimes couldn't make the payments on. That wasn't important, because we Irish looked out for each other. We're all we had in Bridgeport, and we would make it together. This is where my respect began, the son of an old man that was a bond to the community.

"So you admit to the dislike of Blacks and a past criminal behavior toward them. The 14 year old in Horner was Black--did your Hamburgs want their property as well?" Agent Khan interrupts Dick's journey through his childhood.

Dick replies with anger in his voice, "What did we need from a 14 year old? We're not killers. We're not a gang. The Hamburgs have been disbanded for years now, so get your field research right!"

Khan cuts back sternly with a clever look upon his face, as he knew the next question would bore into the inner thoughts of Dick. "As our agency gathers intelligence on all domestic groups, tell me why our information shows that you never disbanded; you were just absorbed into the system--you know, regentrification. We disbanded many youth groups and gangs and the Hamburgs were not one of them, as they were not considered a threat to the way we saw our American society. So Dick, where did your Hamburgs go?"

Dick leaned back in his chair as he began to contemplate the question as it sank into his inner consciousness. Going through his memories, Dick began to recall the rest of his travels throughout his life…

6

In my teens, the neighborhood began to see a ray of prosperity in this country that we didn't have when we first immigrated here. New residents would move in that were of Irish descent only. We would have new recruits as the Hamburgs grew in strength and numbers. Yeah, we were as respected in our neighborhood as any superhero was. We protected what was ours. Anybody that had a problem, we took care of it. Yet it was a rough road to get to this point. The monies that we received from realtors to keep unwanted guests out of our neighborhood so that their property value stayed up was not enough to sustain all of the boys' families. I mean, my old man was all right, but many of the boys struggled as far as their family keeping food on the table. We resorted to other ways of making money such as stealing, robbing, and extortion. We didn't perform those activities in our neighborhood, that would be taking money from those that we struggle with and food out of the mouths of our own families.

We would go to the neighboring Canary neighborhood, where we would rump with its athletic club, the Colts. Canary was a white neighborhood where the families were the descendants of the English that settled this country. They considered themselves better than us and were seen as the true picture of America. Since they had the money, as they displayed, we could use some of it to take care of our land. The English owed the Irish anyway, ya know.

Canaryville wasn't the only neighborhood that we would go to gather funds. We would go to Bronzeville, where the wealthy Blacks stayed. There were no gangs there at the time to oppose us and the police, who were usually from Bridgeport or Canaryville, would never accuse a White man of a crime against a Black in those days. It was a way to get by as we grew good at it. If caught, we were usually let go. In those days Prohibition came and hit our families with a new challenge. The neighborhood bars were boarded and many of the guys' families that worked there needed more income now. We were brothers and we would suffer together. Who knew that prohibition would become the route that we needed to fatten our wallets?

Again Khan interrupted, "So you admit that your gang committed criminal activities that could be considered hate crimes in these times, as well as the corruption of officials and extortion. You were no different from any other gang or terrorist organization."

"Hold on, Khan! You watch your filthy mouth! Where was it that I said murder was involved? We grew out of that. Many of us have respectable jobs, leading respectable lives as productive members of this society. Most of the Hamburgs became city officials and policemen. We give back to this great city more than anybody. As mayor, I have created programs that cater to the communities that we once attacked.

For Blacks we have created employment programs, public aid, and city jobs. What is it that makes you think that we had a hand in the murder of a fourteen year old from the projects? We built those towers to keep the families of the Jews and the Blacks together--what kind of crime is that? Get off my back, Khan, you've got nothing!"

"You don't seem so sure, Dick. There's some intel in between that you don't know I possess. But I'll let you think otherwise. Follow me. I got some guests for you to meet that will make you state otherwise.

Khan walked Dick to the other room to have him sit and wait for these guests. As he was leaving, Khan asked one last question of Dick. "Marinate on this, slick: Hate crimes, extortion, and murder all have a heavy burden of proof, but conspiracy to the activity--what does that carry, preponderance of the evidence? You don't think we have that?"

The Lawrence Inquisition

7

Khan enters the room where Lawrence Malik nick named Law, was being held to begin his questioning. Lawrence was a Black man: 6 feet even, medium complexion of brown tone, weighing in at about 200 pounds of muscle mass that he toned from the time that he did in prison. He had a look of confidence on his face and no fear for authorities such as Khan. He had been in the military before and was trained in hand to hand combat as a ranking Marine. In his mind this was the same as an interrogation if he was ever captured by the enemy during the war. If caught he would provide a mixture of true and false detail while maintaining the secret that the enemy needed. Agent Khan walked around the small room with dim lights, an uncomfortably hard table and chair, and no windows.

Standing, Lawrence watched Khan as he encircled him and said, "You got my lawyer yet?"

Khan spoke. "Lawrence, chairman of the LSD Main 21's, you know why you're here, right? Not the drugs; not the other murders that your gang is associated with; not the intimidation of communities; but one murder in particular."

Lawrence replied, "You talking about that kid in Horner? That wasn't my people that did that. We don't shoot around no kids as a rule against savagery in time of war."

Khan retorted, "I have seen and heard of many occasions where your 'people' have left bodies to rot, mothers to hurt, closed caskets, and hospital bills. How are you going to tell me that your organizations did not do it? Isn't money, macking, and murder what you guys are about, as your literature states?"

Lawrence, remembering, thought, *it wasn't always like that* as he slipped into thoughts of his past.

"When I was a little man in 20th century America, we moved from the South to the North looking for a better way of life. My pops had just returned to us from the war and wanted to experience less prejudice, and the north was the promised land of the Blacks. He laughed. Boy, were we wrong.

"We lived east on 43rd Street, the outskirts of a neighborhood called Bronzeville. Bronzeville was the happening place for Blacks, many of them well-off. My family was poor migrants from the South. We lived outside of Bronzeville, on its west side near the invisible border of the races, State Street. We were constantly warned of the dangers of crossing and playing near State Street, as the whites would hurt or kidnap us. It was just a myth until one day my pops had to stop some white boys from placing me and some friends at the bottom of a pile of sticks and bottles. My pops was fast becoming the man of the neighborhood as a returning war vet. He took no shit from nobody. Ed Jones was his name, but everyone in the 'hood called him Big Ed after he gained some respect. Pops was a factory worker who was out 12 hours a day to take care of his family. We were mainly with moms on the weekdays, with the exception of school. Moms was the glue that kept us all together. She was very family oriented, as was often the case in southern families. That was one good quality that our family would bring to these city folk that would come in handy later.

"Pops would always be concerned about us, as Chicago was a racial hot bed in those days. Racial tensions seemed higher than they were in the south, seeing that the space of the urban area was more concentrated. Every race seemed to be in competition for space to raise their families. Pops gained enough money to move us to a better place, but where were we to go? He didn't quite have enough for Bronzeville homes and the ones he could afford were in or near the white neighborhoods. We knew that was a bust, seeing the commotion on TV about Blacks in white neighborhoods and schools being attacked. An example was the Younger family in that movie, 'A Raisin in the Sun.' That was about a Black family in Chicago, around the time of my youth, trying to move right cross the way in Bridgeport, like we wanted to do. We would stay right here and make 43rd Street our home.

"In the south everyone knew each other and each other's family. That wasn't so in the north, but there was a sense of community within a block radius. Who would have known that the racism and fight for space in the city would bring our blocks even closer?

"One day a little Black girl was found unconscious in an alley near my house. Her parents were found unconscious and beaten up the block somewhere. They had footprints all over them, with purple bruises and blood. The entire neighborhood ran out to see them as the news traveled fast as lightning. My parents were infuriated. At dinner time some neighborhood men and women came over to talk about the racist events that happened. We heard that a gang of white men from the west, either Bridgeport or Canary Ville, did a drive by and hit the family with bottles as they were walking near the invisible border of State Street. The bottle hit the little girl and bounced off her as she fell to the ground. The father then picked up the bottle in great anger and hurled it back at the car which it hit and busted all over. The car did a u-turn and came back. The four men in the car got out and began to beat the family, including the little girl, with a wrench and sticks. The family didn't die, but they were hurt. In tears, my mother told the community about how in the south these things would happen and the mothers would organize a watch system to account for all of the families in the area. She vowed to start one that day with the 43rd Street women. However, pops and the men didn't see that as enough.

"The father whose family was beaten was peaceful. They knew him as Jim, a God-fearing, church-going man that served this country in World War two. Now he was in the hospital. Pops and the others, which included war veterans, would depend on their training as Marines, Army, Navy, and Air Force infantry, along with the weapons they got to defend the neighborhood. No longer were they going to be sitting ducks. Between moms and pops and the solidarity that they learned in the southern protection associations, the 43rd Street block club began. The women enforced a system of watch, accountability, and solidarity; and the men executed the muscle, fraternity, and weapons. The first act was to walk families around the borders, escort women to their cars day or night, and to defensively wait for the drive-bys and mob attacks.

"Moms and the women would gain political respect and job offers from the wealthier Blacks as their reputations traveled. Other neighborhoods wanted to learn their strategy of organization as they became the cement to what many called community, as unity is the root word of community. Pops and his guys would gain great respect from the neighborhood leaders and were fast becoming a force to be reckoned with as time after time, legends of them chasing whites back over the border grew. Yet who knew that these men along with their skill and brawn would become the most organized on the side of both the fight for civil rights and the fight to survive? Either way, they were seen as a threat to the law. It didn't matter what they chose to be whether it was the machine for crime or for justice under the law because the government only seen a threat.

"It was those block clubs as machines for protection and fighters for rights in the cause against realtors not granting space for Blacks based upon race that became what you call my street organizations, the same organizations that served as political machines of the democrats and republicans amongst the Blacks. These same block clubs, as political machines, aided those like Earl B. Dickerson, a Black lawyer who fought against realtors, their tactics, and invisible lines of segregation in the city of Chicago. Such organizations backed Ida B. Wells-Barnett and her husband Charles, another lawyer and members of the nearby Bronzeville area. It was those block clubs whose members filled the ranks of the Moorish Science Temple of America, Black Panthers, Nation of Islam, NAACP, etc. And then there were their children, the Black street organizations…"

Agent Khan interrupted Lawrence's thoughts. "What was better about those days? All you have shown me was that you learned vigilante justice, a dislike for other races, and a disdain for authority from your family. Those are things that lead to activity such as murder. So you're telling me that the block clubs that became known as the gangs you ran still practice vigilante justice today. If this is the case, then it would explain why you or your members killed the young man. It was said that he was found with a gun on his person when the ambulance arrived, but the EMTs reported that a gang member removed it before the authorities arrived.

"So would your defense be self-defense? Were your members worried that he was going to take your life, so before he could they would walk up after school let out and rise from amongst children to take a life in front of small children? Is that the vigilante justice that you speak of? Is that what you learned?" Khan was pointing his finger into Lawrence's chest.

Lawrence's face started to buckle with a mixture of anger and pain. As he rammed his body into Khan in anger, Lawrence shouted, "That's not how I was raised! That's not what I'm about! I'll be damned if you put this one on me, Khan! What do you know any way you Chinky muthafucka!

Huh! What do you know about my organizations?"

Khan replied calmly, "You murder and you kill communities by taking out your own people. You're like a virus that moves into a nice place and sucks out all of the health and resources with your drugs and violence, only to leave the community first in a fever of criminal activity and then to watch it die unless someone else comes in to heal it."

Lawrence asked, "Is that what you think? Is that your intel?"

Agent Khan faced Lawrence eye to eye as agents ran into the room.

Lawrence prepared for combat as Agent Khan demanded that the agents leave them be. Knowing that the government trained Lawrence as well as Khan, the agents would not leave them alone to fight.

Khan yelled at Lawrence, "That's right, show us your disrespect for law and authority, show us the violence, show us what you gang members are about!"

Lawrence, being of high intelligence and street smarts, caught on to what Khan was doing which was playing mind games and proving that he had the capacity to have committed the crime in question.

Calming, Lawrence told Khan, "I'll tell you what we are about."

Lawrence recalled his rise to power and what the youth groups were doing in his late teen years. He talked about the groups that were around and how he became boss.

"Due to great need and want for human advancement--you know, the pursuit of happiness and all that shit--Blacks had organized block clubs all over the city. We were spread out in the city in pockets, surrounded by either the Irish on one side, regular Whites on the other, as far as the South and East side. The West side had Whites in downtown, near west were Italians, near them in Lawndale were Blacks, then Jews, and the Polish had the rest going west. Each race wanted to maintain its own space, and the Blacks--we were just the renters. We could only move to where there was space allowed, not available. There was protection needed in all areas for the Blacks, as we were surrounded. The block clubs became replaced by a larger cause, the Civil Rights Movement.

"All Blacks were fighting for it through organizations, with the exception of the Moorish Science Temple of America and the Nation of Islam, who fought for spiritual, natural, and human rights. The grown-ups left the block clubs due to larger causes such as old age, jail, the Vietnam and Korean wars; police brutality, poverty, death or they moved on to better opportunities. Either way, we youth inherited their legacy--the block club. On the South side we gave them names. There were the 43rd St. Disciples, the 63rd St. Gangsters, the 71st St.

Stones, etc. On the West side there were the Conservative Vice Lords of the Lawndale area near the Polish, the Counts of areas east near the Italians, and smaller groups like the Souls and up and coming High Supreme Gangsters of the Cabrini Green North side which was near Whites of mixed descent.

"Our elders were now in organized groups like the Moorish Science Temple, Black Panthers, NAACP, Urban League, and Religious Movements. The Panthers spearheaded the hot lunch program, the religious movement, moral discipline and educational programs such as tutoring and the Urban League jobs. When they were disbanded or weakened due to government involvement and economic change, we inherited their spirit and their programs. We improved upon the hot lunch program of the Panthers and added the breakfast program, as well. We received monies from the government in the form of grants for aiding in political campaigns. The Blacks were for the Republicans and the Democratic machine for the whites. But the Democrats had been courting us, also. We kept tutoring programs going with such monies and provided scholarships. Like our brothers that returned home from college in organized parties called Greek fraternities, we needed to bond as well.

"These organizations or Block clubs became societies in which we bore our own colors, secret hand gestures, signs and grips. We provided moral support for each other and even allowed female membership, unlike the others. Like the religious men around us, the Stones and Vice lords were impressed by the message of Islam from the Moorish Science Temple of America (M.S.T.A), the N.O.I, and traditional Arab Islam. The Disciples and Gangsters were more impressed by Jewish and Christian morals and teachings, with the Gangsters adding business lore from Robert's Rules of Order. There were also the highly secretive and sophisticated Freemasons, which all of the respected older guys like my father became members of. They sort of ran things as individuals and were not on the forefront but in the center of the great things that went on.

   "We protected and uplifted our neighborhoods. We did things like provide soup kitchens and clothing for the poor or homeless with our government funds, and served as watchmen and body guards for political figures such as Michael King, known as Dr. Martin Luther King, Jr., as he stayed in Lawndale to protest the violation of our rights. We attended Presidential inaugurations by invite, etc. For these purposes the block clubs came together after receiving names and organizing under certain principles. Twenty-one of Chicago's major block clubs came together and created a board that would allow the groups to work together as one inter-community entity, and we did on many of our community projects. We were called the main 21's and I was named Chairman of the board under three kings of the three equally larger groups, the Stones and Disciples. My nickname was given to me, as the chairman was spokesman and keeper of oral laws. My members were so disciplined they called me LAW. Our coalition was termed LSD, or Lords Stones and Disciples. My group at the time was actually the largest, but they couldn't see it at the time since we had all of the outskirts of the city and the north side projects. This is what we did-- this is what we were about--ya dig?"

8

Clapping his hands, Agent Khan applauded Lawrence sarcastically. "You want an award for that piece? All of that, and you guys turned on each other like rabid dogs to fresh meat. Funeral homes have made more money because of your wars. Innocent bystanders have had their lives shortened because of people like you. Kids like Satin Harrington have come to their untimely demises because of you and those like you. Murderers! Fourteen years old!" Khan threw a picture on the desk in front of Lawrence. "He was a member of your gang. So, did you send him out there to get killed? You might as well have pulled the trigger yourself."

Law rebutted, " The discipline I teach is making them go to school, teaching how to put food on their tables, mentoring them on how to be a man, teaching them social, economic, and political development and good hygiene. This is what I enforce upon each and every member, along with respect of elders and authority. I didn't turn the game into what it is today--you did, with the help of the FBI, who took out the leading figureheads, leaving only children to run a criminal empire that is as American as apple pie. The Black man of today is the greatest American product of the twentieth century. So when you point a finger at us, turn your nose up at us, and shake your head saying, 'Look at them,' we say, 'What are you talking about? We MADE IN THE U.S.A.'" Law laughed. "Made in the U.S. muthafuckin A."

Agent Khan walked out of the room, asking two agents to get Law and to follow him as he went down the corridor.

Law asked, "We going home yet Khan?"

"No. I'm taking you to face your destiny. I got enough on you. Oh, and you might want to take off that expensive watch, 'cause where you're going, time will be all you have. You can learn to count as the sun rises and falls on your ass!"

The two agents led Law into a large room where a short and portly Italian man was sitting. "I got someone for you two to meet," Khan said as he left the room.

Concrete and Steel Make a City

9

Since he has been detained in the larger room no one has come in to speak with the Mayor. *How dare they treat me like this?* He thought. In contemplation of the line of questioning executed by Agent Khan, the mayor hears steps as someone is approaching the area. *About time*, he's thinking, as his attorney may be coming to free up his time there so that he may return to city business. The city that works needs its boss he thought as light beamed and spread as the door creaked open.

A Black male of tall stature wearing expensive sunglasses, a Black pin-striped suit, and expensive shoes of Italian leather entered. He was decked out in a gold chain with an interesting pendant. It was shaped like a 6-pointed Star of David, but the ascending triangle was a pyramid. He was also wearing a pinky ring that seemed to direct the light in different directions--or was it his diamond-crested bracelet that mirrored the room? Either way, Dick knew he was definitely no lawyer or Federal agent. So why was he there?

Upon entering the room, Law saw the familiar face of the suited man who was sitting on the cold bench of the large room in the Federal Law Building.

The Mayor, he thought to himself. *Why does the Mayor want to see me? Was the murdered child the biggest issue of the decade? Is it election time or something? Why are they grilling me so hard as to bring the muthafuckin' Mayor into this! This is more serious than other cases that I caught and beat. Never was the Mayor involved. Well, he don't intimidate me, so let's see what the fat man wants.* "Mayor, what brings you here to slum with us little folk?"

Dick gazed at Law to see if he recognized him, with a look of bewilderment as to how Law knew who he was.

With the sound of slight arrogance and defiance in his voice, Law stated to the mayor, "You got some questions for me, too? Imma give you the same answers that I gave Khan--I didn't do it!"

Dick looked upon Law's face as if he was mentally challenged or foreign as he tried to gather understanding of what Law was talking about. It was then that it hit the both of them. They were being questioned for the same crimes, conspiracy and accessory to murder along with a federal hate crime. Looking for more information, they both decided to get to know one another as Law sat leaning against a wall, facing the Mayor.

Law stated, "So, the Mayor of Chicago is up on serious charges with a proposed 'gang leader.' I know we're getting framed." Laughing, Law asked, "How are they possibly going to pull this one off?"

Dick spoke to Law. "You know who I am--who are you?"

"Why Dick, I'm hurt! As many times as I have paid officials and as many fundraisers as I have attended in your presence, you don't know me? Allow me to formally introduce myself-- Lawrence 'the Law' Malik. "

"Lawrence Malik! The head of my city's largest drug empire!"

"No, Law Malik, your friend and investor."

"Why do they have me in here with you? Are they trying to tie me in with crime and street money? They told me it was a murder, but I see this going a whole other way. Hmm, they think that they got something on me, huh? We will see. So, Mr. Law, what is it that they think we have in common here? Murder, accessory, conspiracy, or hate crimes? Do they think you work for me?"

"Work for you?! Man, tight-eyed ass Khan knows the Law don't work for nobody, everybody works for the Law! So, I'm the Mayors muscle now? They think I did the murder for you, huh? Aw hell naw! Well, before I came in Khan said that he would bring someone by that would have something in common with me. He mentioned my background and how I came to be as he gathered from his intel."

Dick said, "Yeah, he pulled the same questions on me."

Simultaneously the two asked, "But what do we have in common?"

10

The two began to think about the past and present ventures. As they became more comfortable with each other, Law asked the Mayor where he grew up.

Dick answered, "35th Street."

Law interjected, "The projects!" with a look of surprise on his face.

"No! Bridgeport."

"Law, Bridgeport. Bridgeport--oh, my pops told me some stories about that place!

"What kind of stories?" asked Dick.

"My pops was a neighborhood hero named Big Ed Jones of the 43rd Street block club, which became known as one of the many factions of the LSD coalition."

Dick exclaimed, "Big Ed Jones! I heard stories of him from my pa. They were enemies that became friends on the basis of business."

Law asked, "What business would that be, Dick?"

"Numbers--the illegal lottery in the neighborhood. Your father also ran a small outfit of handymen that drove for my pa and his friends at the time--the original Outfit. Your father was a Boss in his neighborhood and a legend in his time indeed."

"I can figure how you would see such deeds as honorable, considering the facts that you learned but that's not how my pops gave it to me. He laid it out straight. He told me when I got older that he regretted what he had done for your pops and his Outfit, that he placed his people in danger thinking that people like your pops would allow him equality with them. He was never seen as a leader to them because he was never allowed membership into the Outfit based on race. Pops said that it was like a heart disease to work as a Guinea pig for them when they fought against our people and their advancement. The thing he gives the Outfit credit for was that you provided the Black neighborhoods an illegal way to make money. It was employment, all the same, and they would rather commit that type of suicide than to watch their families starve during the Great Depression and after."

Dick said, "So you're saying that that was a good thing then, right?"

"Hell naw! I vowed that I would never be like my pops and work for guys like that. What you see as working for you I see as working with you."

The room began to heat up as the conversation carried the two in the direction Khan needed them to go. There was a speaker device attached into the walls of the room and a hidden camera where agents could listen in on the conversations. It was not that the information provided was admissible in court; it was that the FBI at the root of the investigation could gather information that would later lead to a bust. The world would never know that this discussion was taped. It was a psychological ploy to place them in the same room as they shared a past and present that would only end up in the buildup of racial tension. Khan was the best psychoanalyst, which made him one of the FBI's top investigators. Now the only thing left to do was throw more gas on the sparks and to create a roaring fire.

Dick stood up in a defensive position as he took disrespect from Law's comments on the actions of his father. Yelling Dick stated, "We didn't owe you nothing, yet Big Ed was looked out for when there were no crumbs to be eaten in the years of the Great Depression and its aftermath.

How dare you throw your ungrateful undertones at such a gesture of good faith! It was your father that betrayed the Outfit and caused his own demise!"

"Yeah, Whitey's favorite defense--blame Blackie! Man, fuck you and yours. We didn't need you or yours handing us shit! You talking like your father did us a favor!" Law erupted into an offensive ball of flame, walking toward Dick with his index finger pointing like a sword. "We ain't immigrant's descendants! We didn't ask to come here to make a life! We are descendants of those brought here to make life better for people like yours! The same way we were used to make life better for people like your Father."

Dick screamed, "Look here, you piece of shit street merchant I'm the king of this city and when you get out of here I will shut your ass down!"

Laughing Law retorted, "You may be the king of a system created to keep you in as its boss, but I run a system that you only connect to in secret. The one that you fail to repair when there are potholes, because you and your henchmen just turn it into ways to make money that returns to you. These streets and its soldiers-- I'm their general whether the color of their skin is red, yellow, black, brown, or white! You and your CPD and their wars against us will remain futile as long as you keep supplying us with drugs and weapons. If you take those away, then we already have enough to fight you with until we make an alliance with some other white man. Look around--your boys in blue ain't here to be your attack dogs, Mr. Mayor. I could whoop your ass right now!"

Dick walked furiously into the path of Law, as if two great generals were about to collide.

Mr. G's Inquisition

11

Khan enters the room, hoping that Mr. G would offer up some look or some words that give a clue as to how his psyche works but finds nothing.

Khan speaks to Giancana, as he only has a smirk to give him. "Mr. G, what's your involvement in this?"

Mr. G pulls out a note pad and ink pen from the pocket of his well-tailored coat and writes down only a few sentences. "I see you're holding my lawyer up, since she beat me here. I know no Mr. G, My name is Miranda - Miranda Rights until my lawyer is present."

Khan speaks to him in a calm manner. "Look, there is nothing to hide, right? You are only here for questions regarding the murder of a 14 year old boy."

Khan tosses the picture of the murder victim on the table in front of Mr. G and it lands under his arm. Mr. G turns in his chair to look at a wall and ignores the picture as he again writes on paper, "Miranda Rights" and slams it on the table on top of the picture as his eyes slowly climb the shirt of Agent Khan, who is now forming a mist of sweat on his face as Mr. G meets his eyes with a hard stare. Khan will take another approach here.

Khan said, "O.K. I'll talk and you will listen. There are movies glorifying scum like you. America loves a gangster, but I got a different picture of you. We've investigated your family for years and have even infiltrated it. We've been members of your Outfit and have taken it down to help it turn into the weak and shabby organization that it is today. I'm going to tell you the story of your family and its reign of terror on this great city. Like other immigrants around the

U.S., you came here in search of a better life, to taste this sweet democracy. But you only brought your sour ways from your old country, as criminals like your father brought their Mafioso ways with them along with a trail of criminal records and activity. You thought that you could do the same in Chicago as in New York. But Chicago was different for the Italians, wasn't it? It was further from the harbor where immigrants came into New York. It was a powerful city that worked when you got here and there were not nearly as many Italians here as there were in New York. Your family worked in hard labor jobs such as construction, the steel factories over on Taylor Street, and the fish factories over on Lake Street, along with the Canal docks. They were hard-working citizens that moved over into the neighborhood just west of downtown and the Canals to be closer to jobs. You were all surrounded but that little piece of land that you all carved for yourselves became known as the Little Italian Village. The property that your family lived on was owned by Jews who rented to you out of favors owed to you and your fathers as good workers. You had a little help from New York on real estate connects with the Jews and bought in as a race. No self-respecting Italian immigrant was a criminal in Chicago. There was no easy route, and in Chicago one worked hard for their earnings, hence the name the City That Works rather than the Second City as it was once called."

12

Khan continued, "The Village was small and all the Italians stuck to themselves, as their culture was their own. You would form athletic clubs like the rest to keep your community full of your culture. No outsider could get in to marry into your original Italian blood, to spoil your culture. Italy would survive as an outstanding entity in America. The fathers would work their asses off to keep food on the tables and clothes on your back, while the mothers would preserve the culture and pass it to you all daily. After work your father and the boys from Italy would go out and have a drink. That was, until one day they were told that the bars were closed. Liquor was prohibited. They were infuriated. How is this great democratic government going to tell grown men that work hard for it daily that they can't enjoy a little leisure? What happened to life, liberty, and the pursuit of happiness? This action became a way out as time got hard for the hard-working immigrants. The market crashed and jobs were becoming scarce also.

"Alcohol would become a booming multi-million dollar business for your father and his friends as the bootlegging industry became the labor that would provide the Little Italian Village with prosperity and power. Your father would have liked to monopolize on it, but as I said earlier, the Italian population in Chicago was not as great as New York then. You shared neighborhoods surrounded by Blacks, Jews and Pols. Unlike the powerful mob of New York, your father and his friends had to settle and share the power of the bootleg industry with the Irish and the Jews. The Blacks were hired as your runners, but you kept them out of the real money. You had to share the power with the Irish and Jews already, but you would be damned if you did with the niggers. At least you were stronger than the Niggers, right?"

Khan watched as Mr. G began to squirm in his chair uncomfortably. Mr. G moved around in his chair, as his facial expression showed anger and the effort of suppressing it. Khan would attack what all men alike seemed to hold dear-- his pride and ego.

Khan went on talking. "Weaker than their brothers in New York, the Italians of Chicago buckled under the pressure of losing battles with the Irish, who had a political hold on Chicago, and the Jews, who held great resources such as jobs and real estate. Your father folded and formed an alliance with the stronger enemy Irish and Jews, which was termed the Outfit. The most famous of you was Al Capone. Your image went right down the drain as the hard-working Italian immigrant turned into the manipulative Italian gangster. You would murder and kill whomever you could to maintain your status quo. You finally gained power in the Outfit, as powerful as your New York brothers. They would offer their assistance to the Chicago Italians because you proved yourselves. Through cunning plans you took over the outfit and became the leader to the Irish and Jews.

Tell me something, wouldn't you like to hear the story of the hard-working Italian immigrant rather than the cowardly Italian that bombed, shot, or tortured defenseless and unarmed people for property, power, and the criminal racket? Or are you as murderous as your father and his gang? That 14 year old was only a child, a child of America, and just like the many children that your father killed when he separated families. Do me a favor, G., and tell me you are as weak as your father and his people and you had that child shot because you wanted his property or because his boss crossed you or simply because you are an animal like your people have been depicted in these murderous mob movies."

13

"Shut up! Shut up! Shut up, you spineless Asian pig! I've had enough of you!" ranted Mr. G "Let me tell you about my father and my people. We gave jobs to those in our community when this country could not provide it for its citizens. We not only provided jobs for our own but the Blacks, Asians, and Hispanics as well. What crime is it to take care of your own like Malcolm X said, by any means necessary, huh? How respectable is a man that can't feed his family? Today we provide scholarships and philanthropic services to people of all races. Today we are not fighting for blocks of property but to sell them to all regardless of race. Today my unions and corporations are hiring those of all races. We are no longer in the field and on blocks working to intimidate so that we are on top. We do the same thing as America does when it goes into other countries for war--protect our way of life! We ain't out there killing no kids!"

Khan was ready to take G. to the next phase of his questioning. "You will talk, G. Think about this one question for a second... What do you have in common with those you are about to meet? Oh, by the way, the witness to the murder has arrived."

He was going to take G. to a room where his past indiscretions would collide with his present. To a room where the lies would all come out as war would arise between the greatest powers of Chicago...

Three Minds One Life

14

The door swings open with great force as two agents rush in to wedge between the colliding walls of anger that were Dick and Law. The agents saw them face to face, yelling at the top of their lungs, as if at any second blows would be exchanged. One agent began to escort Dick from the large room to another room when Agent Khan, who was en route with Mr. G, had stopped him at the door.

"What are you doing, agent?"

"Sir, these two were at each other's throats and to prevent a liability to our headquarters, I decided to separate them, sir."

I gave no such order Agent.

"But sir, this here is the Mayor of Chicago; he doesn't deserve to be attacked by some dope dealer."

Khan spoke with great authority. "Agent, I'm going to tell you something that will advance your knowledge greatly. All of these men are here for one common purpose--as suspects in federal charges such as hate crimes, conspiracy to commit murder, accessory to murder, and the murder of a 14 year old American youth, a youth that never got to see what prom was like; never got to see what sex was like; never got to see his children; never got to spread his family gene; never got to go to college."

His eyes misted over, Khan's anger was revealed as he continued, "Do you have children,

Agent? Because I do. Do you remember 14 and up? 'Cause I do. Would you like to see your children all live past such a young age? Then you treat men like this as they are! Animals-- intelligent but beastly and instinctive animals! They are all equal here, Agent."

The agent let go of Dick as if all of the words of his superior sunk in. The Agent's eyes were aglow as the look on his face became very somber. He could feel the pain at the loss of a child of America. The agent tugged Dick into the direction of the room interior. Khan lightly shoved Mr. G into the large room as well. With the slam of the door, the three were left in a room with only each other to face. Law gave Dick a hard stare as they both kind of glanced over at the new guy. Their eyes would meet in a lock again as Law suddenly charged at Dick.

The Witness

15

Khan quickened his step to the elevator of Chicago's 24- story federal building, where the FBI was stationed. Speaking to the other agent as he saw the importance of the matter that they were traveling so fast to get to, Khan said, "We have a break in the case that may put pressure on those guys. They have been loosened up; their minds are cluttered with anger and bewilderment. This is why I left them in that bullpen together. If you place three male, pride-driven animals of the same species in any foreign environment where the quarters are close, the leader will reveal himself through dominance of territory. Along with that, the weakest will be exposed. With that exposure we will have our snitch."

The other agent responded, "That's smart thinking, sir, I see why you wanted them there. That's why you are our top interrogator."

"Yes, agent, but there is a downside to this."

"What's that, sir?"

"Well, you've heard of John Locke?"

"Yes, sir."

"He had a philosophy in his Declaration of the Rights of Man that in an environment human kind could either perish in anarchy or come together in a society to survive through a social compact or contract with each other. We may be doing ourselves a great injustice by putting those three masterminds together. Yet, it's a chance I'm willing to take."

The agent replied, "If it is like what Thomas Hobbes said as a counter to Locke, 'Mankind is inherently evil and will commit instinctive acts,' then the men may trample over each other until the stronger one is revealed, as you stated. As Darwin said, only the strong survive."

Delighted with the stimulating intellectual conversation, Khan replied, "My, aren't you the psychosocial learner, and here I am with the PhD in Psychology with emphasis on the criminal mind. Where did you attend school, agent?"

" University of Illinois, sir."

Well, I'm a Harvard scholar myself. Let me guess, you got a B.A. in Speech Communications with a background in Psychology and your M.A. was in Criminal Justice. You graduated Magna Cum Laude of your class and received many honors. Correct?"

Looking astonished at the level of skill Khan possessed, the agent pondered how Khan knew such things without looking into a file. *All he does is look into the person and he has a master profile on them.*

Then the agent returned a shot at Khan. "You were Cum laude of your class with a degree in Psychology and a background in Sociology. Your M.A. was in Criminal Justice and your Ph.D. in Psychology."

A little impressed, Khan looked at the agent and asked his name, as he was new to the investigative unit.

"Agent Pride, sir."

"Well, Agent Pride, you were right in many areas, but my undergrad was a double major of Psychology and Sociology with a minor in human development and I graduated Summa Cum Laude, all after working as a City cop. My M.A. was in Clinical Psychology with a certificate in speech communication. My PhD was in Sociology, where I wrote a dissertation on the effects of human consciousness on behavior. Or as I saw it, psychology's effect on sociology and how this in turn affects human development. After this, my research got me a bid with the FBI's investigative unit--after I finished my degree while serving in the Navy."

The conversation came to a halt as the two neared the corridor where the witness was waiting. The two walked down the hall of the third floor, where witnesses were brought a safe distance from defendants and those in question, who were held on the 24th floor. To keep the witnesses' identities safe, none of the doors on the 3rd floor had windows, unlike those on the 24th floor, where all those in question of criminal activity could be kept under watch at all times. Dismissing Agent Pride to attend to the three men in question, Khan reached for the door to press the entry code on the protected oak door. Only certain agents possessed the entry code to those doors, which was the only way in or out of a room with a witness.

16

When the door opened, the large eyes of a 15 year old teen peered up as his mother looked on protectively as she sat next to him. The witness did not look scared in the foreign environment of a federal building. The room that the witness was in had a large oak desk with a leather seat with wheels on one side. On the other side of the desk were plush suede seats and palm plants. The lights were perfect as the sun shone through the well-lit windows. The air was nice. The room was comfortable.

Khan extended his hand to the mother of the youth first as a gesture that he respected her and that she was in charge as the child's guardian. "Agent Khan Chi Ins, ma'am, pleased to meet you."

The mother met his hand as a gesture of trust and respect returned. "A-a- Ada Gardner."

After releasing Ada's hand, Khan turns and reaches out to the teen. "Agent Khan Chi Ins of the FBI."

The teen returned reluctantly but clearly, "Michael Gardner."

Already Khan was analyzing their profile and had come to a quick judgment that the woman was a hard working single mother raising between 5 and 9 children and was protective. She was strong as the role of both mother and father was filled by her. As for the 15 year old teen, he came off as timid and lacking trust in non-familial authority. He was a teen of the streets all right. But there was something about him that Khan saw in himself at his age that intrigued him. Noticing that the teen would most likely want to hide his street life from his mother, Khan asked Ada if she could trust him with her child, as he needed no reluctance to the truth from the child.

Of course the mother, in protection of the child, said with authority, "No!" And with the neck rolling as a gesture of sassy seriousness she added, "Whatever you can say to him, you can say to me!" She then placed her arm around the clean-cut and neatly dressed Black teen of approximately 5 feet 6 inches, 138 pounds and eyes that reflected the look of great innocence.

Kahn began to tell the mother the importance of Michael's testimony and that he was only being questioned. Khan went on to say that the teen's testimony could lock up criminals that could have killed her child and may endanger the lives of other children. "Ma'am, these guys are powerful predators and will and can hurt others. I'm not going to lie to you and tell you that you and your family won't be in danger if his story checks out and such men of power are found guilty based on his testimony. I can promise you that we will be there to protect you all and can provide you a new life in our witness protection program. This program will give you a new identity, will provide you with money to pay bills, a job, educational opportunities—"

"-- A new credit score," Ada interrupted.

Khan laughed. "Sure, that will come along with your new social security numbers."

Even with the ice being broken between Ada and Khan, she was still a little reluctant. "Con, that's your name, you sound like one. I'm not placing my son in such danger. How can he enjoy such a new life if he is dead?"

A cloud of seriousness and mistrust once again took over the room as the laughter faded.

Khan, even more somber, leaned in and looked into the eyes of Ada as he sat on top of the desk before her and Michael, and said," Ada, isn't his life in danger if he goes back to the projects anyway? Isn't there still a war out there? Don't you still struggle?"

The child looked up at his mother and said, "Go ahead, mom, I trust him. I'll talk to him."

Ada looked at Michael as if his words carried great weight with her, as if he was more than a son, but was also a good friend. This is what

Kahn saw that reminded him of himself--the sign of a leader of a broken family, that of an alcoholic suffering from great depression. He was the young family leader and Khan would expect him to be more cunning and intelligent than his innocent eyes let on. The mother began to get out of her seat as Khan arose to unlock the door with his combination on the key pad.

"Thank you, Ada. Make a right and go down that corridor and you will see a waiting room with a few televisions and snack machines."

Ada looked Khan up and down as if her eyes were communicating with Khan's. The look was a warning as Ada only said, "Hmm," rolled her eyes and walked away. Now Khan was alone with Michael.

"Look, I checked your background and you have no juvenile record; are the top of your class as a straight 'A' student; participate in sports and gymnastics; work after school as well as tutor. As a witness you cannot have any blemishes on your character, as the defense will be strong and will attack you. I need to know more about your background to prepare you for what is to come."

"Aiight," Michael responded.

"So tell me about you, the whole truth, Michael. I need everything."

Bull Pen

17

Law and Dick suddenly found themselves on the ends of the left and right hands of a tall, dark-haired white male in a tailored, pin-striped, beige suit.

Mr. G said, "I don't have a bone to pick with either of you but this ain't gonna help none of us." Staring into both of their eyes, G stated," Don't you see his mind game?"

Law's muscles began to relax as he had a look of discovery on his face and finished off Mr. G's statement. "Divide and conquer."

Dick stated, "So we are here on purpose. He has a plan?"

As he backed away Dick stated, "After all my years in politics, I should be used such tactics. My old man told me about such tactics--dirty politics, huh? He told me that the FBI pulled such tactics to rope off election bids in the late '50's and early '60's. He told me that cities like Chicago were power centers and were like water droplets in this great ocean called the U.S. of A. My father taught me that when it came politics those that got elected controlled the monies and powers afforded to the FBI. The FBI was created during the time that the Democrats had power and were sustained by such a power. Then the Democrats were more conservative White Americans; hence the FBI was a more conservative institution and preferred conservative policy. Anything leftist was too close to the fascists, zealots, dictators, and socialists/communists which the FBI investigated to protect our country. With that being in mind, the interest of the American (white) majority was also perpetuated.

All of this came to fruition in 1968, when the Black Stone Rangers held an election boycott that cost the Democrats dearly. Then the Blacks were still a great force behind the Republican ticket. This boycott had such effects that in '69 when my old man was mayor, he promised to deliver Chicago to the Democratic nominee Hubert Humphrey, who lost Illinois to Nixon. Such an action led to the demise of my old man as Mayor, seeing that the president that he openly opposed gained power--it was only a matter of time.

Looking at Law, Dick stated, "It was then that my old man saw people like you as a threat to his power and pledged to wipe such organizations out with his organization, who were now employees in one of the most powerful enforcers of law, the CPD. Such organizations were a political power that could turn the tide of voting any way, but the old man didn't want to get rid of them, he wanted to use them to his advantage.

Right after that, Blacks became part of the Democratic machine instead of the Republican. We do it in politics; now it's being done to us." Dick shook Mr. G's hand. "How ya been, John?"

Mr. G replied, "Better before this shit, Dick."

Law looked surprised that they knew each other until he realized who the man in the suit was. Mr. Giancana and the mayor? *Whoo-hooo, this is headlines. Oh, I know I'm fucked up now. They got me on charges with two of the most powerful men in the city, one seen as a criminal for making payoffs and contracting his close associates and their family and the other a corporate mogul and leader of Unions with his own labor and construction firms who give money to the mayor's campaigns in return for contracts.*

"Mr. G, for a street cat, you sure know business and politics."

"How ya been, Law" asked Mr. G as he shook his hand.

Law replied, "Small world, huh, J.R.?"

Surprised, Dick said, "You two know each other?"

"You really think I'm a petty drug dealer, huh, Dick. You may have heard of my construction company--Millennium Monarch Builders, Inc. Yeah, we ask you for contracts every fiscal year only to be out bid by some White company or maybe a friend of yours like J.R. here."

"Why do you call him J.R.?"

"He's John Giancana, Jr. It's short for Junior. My companies have been doing work through small contracts from J.R. for years. He's the reason that we can receive a piece of this pie that you slice him out for whatever he does for you. We are still the manpower of you whites today," Law said, laughing. "Just like with my daddy and yours during the numbers or the campaigns. We are connected by more than one way. Our fathers knew each other and had done business with each other for some time before they were separated by one thing or another. Maybe if we can go over our connections we can find out why we are really here or how he thinks he has us."

The three sat down and began to talk.

18

Classrooms With and Without Walls

Revisiting his youth Michael began to speak to Agent Khan, Here's how it all started: Facing the flag, the entire class of 1991 states in unison, "I pledge allegiance to the flag of the United

States of America, and to the republic for which it stands, one nation, under God, indivisible, with liberty and justice for all."

Looking around one sees one small classroom, boys and girls 12 years of age, one teacher--one constant environment that won't change for a year. It is 9 a.m., homeroom time. As I am one of the first in the class and at my desk, the regular routine is the same every year. In come the smart girls that happen to be cheerleaders: Stacy (I think she is a little chunky yet a total package), T.T (this girl had lips that seemed to be both a gift and a curse), Christina (sexy chocolate and my rival for all academia), Kara (now she had a flawless ass on her, with a face to match). Now enter some of the guys who are part of the basketball team that happens to also be mainly composed of those with high academic scores: Skip was the top of the cool group and was also intelligent; Hawk, a regular comedian and partial bully if you let him and an all around athlete, who was also intelligent yet was a follower; Joe, a regular comedian and average student; Big Man, a smart top-contending comedian, strong willed, man's man; and Rick T, a comedian with the coolest swagger of all time or so he thought.

Yep, this is the cream of the crop but it doesn't stop here. The late people arrive in class like they just don't want to be there. I mean, I saw all of them early at free breakfast and at the playground so why they're always late to class, I have no idea. Yet they make up the rest of the who's who of school. Let's see... entering is J.D., a comedian, gang member of the Black Disciple (B.D.) class, who held low grades but high common sense and street credibility. R.P. was a gang member, not too bright but a little funny and tried to be too funny and wanted to be a bully and a tough guy since he was also a BD like J.D. Yet R.P. was too scrawny to put fear into anyone.

You see, there are 60 or more teens in the area, with two teachers present. From what I can remember the social construct was the Cool group which was made up of the Athletes, comedians, cheer leaders, and the gang members-as the top, then the nerds (text book and/or computer geeks) at the middle, the bums (most impoverished and lower hygienic), and lames (not real/try too hard to fit in) at the bottom. Yep, this is Dett Elementary class of 1991, 6th grade. And where do I fit in all of this? Well, I am somewhat all of the above with the exception of lame, because I never cared what they thought of me. I'm a freethinker. I was called a bum because my hygiene was not the best and I didn't dress the most color-coordinated. The other students teased me and mainly said, "How come you don't dress like your sister and brother?"

As a leader and freethinker, I didn't care about their ranting and was oblivious to fashion trends. But Skip would always tell them that I was cool and just needed to pick up on my gear a little. Was that an invitation to the cool group? I wasn't gonna hold my breath. See I am confident in who I am. Not only am I the top of my class academically, I've always been a champion roaster and no one, not even the girls, get spared from my wrath. To top all of that off, I am one of the champion fighters in our grade so who wants it? Yeah, I thought not, no one wants to see me.

Wait, hold on for a second, right before class starts and before the teacher sits, everyone wants to play the dozens. Randy is looking around with a smirk on his face and sees Big Man at the back of the class and says loudly in the direction of the class, talking about Big Man's large forehead, "Shouldn't you be in the front of the class since you are the head?"

Big Man shoots back with a reply about Randy being seen as the class reefer head, "Maybe this is the front and you too high to notice."

Hee-Hee-Hee. Man, I'm laughing loud already as they both turn to me and Randy says," I know you ain't laughing," he says, "looking like master splinter from the sewer."

And Big Man says, "Yeah, the turtles need your help," as both they laugh.

OHHHH naw y'all ain't! Then I return with full enthusiasm, "Hey, y'all," as I call the class to attention. "When Randy and Big Man got up this morning instead of changing they clothes, they changed they faces to uglier (ha-ha-ha). Randy look like Mum Ra (in a melodic tone) and Big Man is like his ugly-ass dawg Ma Mutt. Plus, they mamma so bald head when she sleep at night her head slips off of the pillow."

The entire class laughs at them as I sit down quickly, with the almost psychic feeling that someone of authority is approaching.

The teacher would enter and give the class the most piercing look, saying, "What's so funny? Y'all must have seen y'all test scores."

As we quiet down, he says, "Aw, ain't no laughter now."

This was amongst the best times that we would have in our lives, because we would go separate ways once we left the classroom to go home. Yeah, one of the safest and most fraternal places for us was school, but that all changed once we got out.

Right across the street from school was a void where purses were being snatched, kids were getting beat up, sometimes there were gunshots, but beyond all of that was home. Moms and Dads would be waiting with a nice snack or food cooking; siblings waiting to beat you at a video game or something; friends waiting to go outside and play with you. Usually, the gang members would go with the gangs and the rest of my class would go to different after-school programs. The athletes would go to Chicago Commons for sports on a daily basis, while some of the class would go to work. I go to the nuns for games, homework help, snacks, and religious studies on a daily basis. Monday through Friday my schedule was as follows: I go to Chicago Commons for community outreach and job training from 2:30 – 4:30, then the nuns after school from about 5-7 p.m., then on Wednesdays from 7-9 p.m. at the "white church"; Thursday 7-9 at "club," another Christian youth center; and Sundays at St. Stephen's church.

You might think, "Man, this guy was busy, was he trying to avoid gangs or were there problems at home?"

You would think that my mom let me go to all of those activities plus church because I was the Omen. Yet, the truth of the matter is that I attended on my own. But don't get it twisted; I was not trying to avoid the gangs. No sir, the gangs were something that I wanted to be a part of. It was the most bonded portion of the neighborhood outside of the home and school. It seemed to have powerful members that commanded respect, the girls liked them, they seemed cool, and there was always something that attracted me to bond with others. Yet nothing was stronger than my urge to be part of something bigger and possibly greater than myself that held secret knowledge in it that I could master. This would explain why I was in all of those church organizations at one time, the brightest in school, and soon to be one of the brightest in street knowledge (common sense), which was a realm that I hadn't mastered as of yet.

19

Agent Khan, as an expert analyst, was thinking to himself that Michael's need to belong to something outside of his nuclear family may have stemmed from the absence of his father. He had heard nothing about the natural presence and existence of a father in the entire story. As he listened on, he would interrupt Michael with the question, "You wanted to belong to something outside of your family--how many siblings do you have and where is your father?"

Mike replied, "I have 8 siblings and my father--he comes around here or there."

Khan noticed that Mike held no ill will towards his father. He asked another question, "Were any of your siblings in a gang?"

"Two of my older brothers are Gangster Disciples from the Cabrini Green projects."

Khan asked," Do they live with you or spend a lot of time with you?"

Mike replied, "No"

Agent Khan thought privately that the older male influence in Mike's life seemed shaky and pondered as to it being a reason that he joined the gang. He needed more information on his witness, as his background may be more singed than he needed it to be. He needed the child's testimony to stand.

Khan asked, "Tell me how you became involved with the GD's?"

With a look on his face that said this was going to be a hell of a journey, Mike took a deep breath and began to speak.

"My world changed at the point of 6th grade. My family was evicted from the projects, moving me from my neighborhood and my connections. We moved from the Notorious Henry Horner Projects to the K-town section of Chicago. K-town was the old Polish neighborhood that Martin Luther King lived near and wanted to help desegregate, along with Marquette Park. It was originally called K-town because it is a 2 mile stretch of streets named after those honored by the Polish peoples whose last name begins with K. Beginning with Kasimir Pulaski all streets going west were names like Kolmar, Karlov, Keeler, Kostner--you get it. Going to the public park in K-Town, you would see at least 50 people in a large circle on certain nights. I would inquire as to who it was and was told the GD's by my new-found associate who was a member. I told my associate about my oldest brother who was in jail now for putting in work in Cabrini Green by taking over areas further north for the High Supreme Gangsters GD's. They gave him the name Maniac for his work. Maniac told me stories about GD which sounded like those mobster and cowboy stories on T.V.

"My associate admired me having a legacy in my family and asked if I was interested in becoming a member. I said yes after the thoughts of my brother's heroism of protecting his 'hood was in my head. What happened next would change my mentality forever. It started with attending a business meeting and being introduced to the co-ed brotherhood. They asked me why I wanted to become FOLKS and what I knew about it. They were astonished at what I knew from my two brothers and made the decision that it was in my heart. They began with giving me the rank of a wannabe. Then there was a system of becoming a full member."

20

Mike continued, "It was different than how I had heard it from my older brother when he became a GD. He was jumped into his initiation or what you call hazed. He told me stories of flashlights, blows to his body, and lectures passed down to him and all gangsters before him. I, on the other hand, had only received the watered-down version of that initiation. The rules were changed. I had gone through trials and oral tests. I had to attend every meeting to ascertain what was going on with the organization and if I wanted to become a real part of it. I moved up the rank of Shorty G, a new fledgling soldier.

"Being looked at for membership, I would learn secrets as to wars, be given small pieces of literature to learn, and knowledge about murders and how things are in this day as a wannabe or potential. I was watched daily to see if I could perform one of the most valuable tasks needed of a member of GD--keeping my mouth shut, keeping secrets about crime, and knowing the rules and regulations given me on paper to study as assessment.

"After being watched for a year I was ready and invited to a meeting. After reciting all of the lit that I was given, along with further knowledge that I had obtained through my persistence in picking the minds of the elders for more knowledge, I was then given my new rites. I attended a special business meeting in the presence of all the leaders, which was only privy to members. I would be given the ranks and identities of all of the neighborhood's members to protect as long as I was a member and then would be given the once secret, now publicly known grip of the GDs. I was told that some of the signs and grips were made public through the aftermath of some thing called 'Coin tell Pro.' Along with that, the secret identity and lives of the new urban societies were exposed to the public through the media. Such rites made me feel cheated out of receiving the greatness that my oldest brother had told me about."

Interested in learning more about the organization that the FBI had studied, Kahn asked Mike about the story that his big brother told him. With reluctance and taking a deep breath first as a bit of reverence appeared in his eyes, Mike began to speak stating, first of all I ain't no snitch but in order to protect the Brothers of the Struggle I will let you know some things that will help you to see us in our true form.

21

"Okay, picture this. You are totally in the dark. You don't remember the last time that it was so dark in your life but this darkness makes you very nervous. You don't know what is going to happen because you can't see the course before you and you yearn for the safety of the light. You do know what is outside of the place that you are in and some of the people that you knew that await you in the light. The cold wind of a Chicago winter is upon you but all you feel is heat in the air and even sweat at your brow. Your stomach is in a knot and you jump even more when you hear a powerful voice come forth from a distance in the darkness.

"The voice says, 'You are here of your own free will and can only proceed as such. You know where the door is and can turn and leave now or go forward into the rest of a new life in our family.' You had been thinking about this moment for some years now and finally get the chance to be in a position to join the ranks of great respected men and women around you. Naturally you have courage, dedication, and a strong will and only wish to proceed.

"You jump as the strong but familiar voice is projected through the darkness again and says, 'Whatever you do and whatever is done to you, focus on the sound of my voice and mine only. Trust in what I say and walk only a straight path when I reveal it to you. If you follow any other path you will enter parts unknown to our bond and may never return to the path of greatness that we all follow.' There is a thunderous clap from the area of the voice!

"You see before you a path between two rows of lights that seem to be flashlights held by a long line of people. In the complete dark, the windy and long corridor has the appearance of a landing strip of an airport. The noise level rises as you take your first step; the temperature of the room also rises. The noise level is increased with sounds of screams, banging bottles, clapping sticks, and the sounds of many human voices. As you step between the lights you are pushed from side to side violently by unseen forces at first as if they were trying to keep you from moving forward in a straight path. Yet you trudge on. You hear other strange voices saying things like 'you ain't gone make it,' 'you weak,' 'you don't want this,' "turn back," 'save your life,' etc... As you move forward things get more violent as you feel a sharp blow to your side, 'Oww, what was that?' Then another!

"You hear the familiar voice say, 'Don't panic, do you want to go back? Because the road will only get worse and you will lose your life by the end of this path.'

"You hesitate to think, but the forces begin to move you again. There is a sharp blow to your head and then, someone swiftly pulls you back from your path--this was unexpected! You fall; now you are getting dragged and hit from all directions. You feel that you are getting dragged from the lights of the path off to another place.

"The voice says 'Get up, you can do it. Find the path. Those forces can only harm you if you don't want the straight path.' You feel a little pain but immediately find a rush of adrenaline.

You tell yourself, *I ain't going out like this*. You fight your way through until you are back on the path.

The voice is continuous now, you can hear it reciting 'Yea, though I walk through the valley of the shadow of death...' The lights are flashing everywhere now; you are being hit from left to right, pushed from side to side, feeling pain from all directions, but you refuse to fall down and be pulled back. It is noisier as you hear the sound of other voices shout out obscenities against you, telling you that you are about to die soon. Now you feel liquid drip down your head in great volume as you move on. Man, is it that hot in here?

"You move on; the voice is upon you. You are almost right there but right before you touch the voice, something or someone jumps directly in your way on the path and grabs you, saying that you will not pass. You wrestle with them; you think how strong they must be as you are totally losing ground with them.

"The voice yells, 'Don't give in--it is only one man and he is in the way of your destiny. Fight! Fight for a better way- fight for your family- fight for your life!' Now you feel others joining the one that was before you and all of a sudden you are overwhelmed by them all. You feel pain but don't cry out.

You hear the voice say strongly, 'If everything belongs to everyone, then everyone can take everything, including someone else's life. We must bind together in a social contract for the survival of mankind.'

"Then you feel arms embrace you and pull you out of the abyss of pain and people. and as the hitting stops, the lights suddenly come on. You are in awe as you see the large number of strong men and women about you that you fought to get through. The man with his arms around you that pulled you out says with the familiar voice that guided you out, 'Disciple is the root word to discipline, and a disciplined spirit is what helped you through. God is what saved your life, and we your family are who went through it with you.'

"You are overwhelmed with the feelings of ease that it is over and joy as you have passed on to a new life with those respected in the neighborhood. You made it through the death walk. You are alive. As you wipe the sweat from your brow, you see it is red; it is mixed with blood. The new people around you welcome you with hugs and handshakes as you are told that blood is never the only thing that binds Black people; it is also culture and spirit.

"The leader then ends saying, 'This experience you will never forget; you are a disciple now and one of nations within a nation.'

22

Kahn was astonished at the ritual that he just heard. This was not in the FBI files that he read. Yet, Khan wondered and asked Mike, "Out of all the good in your heart, what would drive you to join a gang that commits murders, sells drugs, and other crimes?"

Michael replied, "I am no criminal, sir. What they taught me was valuable to me. You would teach your own children what we learn."

Khan replied, "And what's that?"

Mike began to speak about literature class that they had to attend. In Literature class the teacher would teach us…

Lesson From the Lit (literature) Teacher

23

"One major part of joining a Chicago Urban Secret Society was the learning of history and symbolism though lectures and self discipline through memorization. There were two ways to advance in this society, one through courage under leadership and fire and the other though intellectual advancement in the lessons and the proper execution of them. These societies were all set with teachers that give the laws and history both orally for the deeper secrets and in writing for the laws. The laws were given to every member to serve the republican portion of this direct democracy, modeled after America as a democratic–republic. These lessons are what get you past the vast neighborhoods and allow other factions of your society to recognize you and allow rival societies to respect you.

"Once you exchange the secret grip, you will be brutally questioned as to your authenticity by the knowledge that you retain. If you don't retain enough knowledge then you may be punished either as a 'false–flagger' (even though you know that you are real) or you will be treated like a low level member, a foot soldier or zombie. This is not the way our set of the society likes to be portrayed, so you are to study and study hard before you reveal to any person that you are one of us.

Along with this is the paying of monthly dues and taxation for the advancement of the society. If you cannot afford the financial responsibilities, we will have to make a way so that they get paid for you. Along with that if you ever falter in your economic status we are to make a job for you to provide for self and family by any means necessary. So, make all meetings or as many as possible, because if we see that you want to be idle in your ways and not work your way up, you will be treated like your position, the bottom, the dirt of the ground. If there is no struggle there is no progress. As a lesson to this, a lit teacher would tell you to Follow Our Last Kings Scroll (F.O.L.K.S).

"The literature teacher then goes on to explain, 'This scroll is entitled the rules of engagement and it explains the rules of the street gang society as compared to greater secret societies which were its role model. What the initiate will get out of this scroll is a greater understanding that street gangs are actually small secret societies which provide fraternal bonds for the survival of urban populations as an adaptation to an environment that is often unseen by the upper portions of the U.S. economic scale. This scroll is your initiation into secret societies from the bottom up.'"

Khan interrupted again with a question to Mike. "So what happened that led up to the events of the murder at Horner? What were you doing over there? Why is it so hostile?"

Mike's eyes began to develop a look of great sadness and anger. Khan sat back in a chair, as it looked as if the story was about to become more interesting. He asked Mike if he needed a break or wanted something to drink.

Mike answered, "A pop--you got orange?"

Khan got on the phone to ask for a large pizza with orange pop to be sent to the witness chambers. Anticipating the arrival of pizza and pop, Mike began to tell the story of Horner.

A Trip to Horner

24

"Skip and the rest of my friends would morph into a culture entirely opposite to the path that the school and community centers have placed them on. You see, the boys on the team had never had direct problems from the BDs with the exception of what went on in the neighborhood that concerned their family members. Things like robbery, rape, and intimidation had plagued our families but as hoopers, they were often seen as economic gain for the BDs. The BDs that had money would hire the players for their urban league teams and would often gamble thousands against other leaders of organizations called 'gangs.'

This all came to an abrupt halt, as community outreach workers by the names of Hen and John had other plans for the guys. Hen and John would come to the school to get the fellas and take them directly to Chicago Commons to practice. Hen would shield the guys from the BDs, often at the unseen threat of his life. Yet everybody in the neighborhood respected Hen. He was the embodiment of a modern Fred Hampton. He was cool since Grammar School, an athlete in High School, a ladies' man, a graduate of Junior College at the time; and had worked with many of the teens in the neighborhood as an advisor and guide through life. Hen would do what he could to make sure that every teen that he helped received the advantages that he worked for in life. He would teach the teen males that they don't have to be statistics and that they can make the difference. Hen had helped lames to be themselves and become cool, the impoverished to get jobs, the sons and family members of gangs to get out of jail when police brutality was involved, etc. There was so much influence that he held. He would even quash gang wars.

"On the other hand, John, he was more laid back than Hen. I mean he was an athlete and all, but he wasn't the sweat suit type like Hen. Naw, John was a suave, stylish, one-woman man with a genteel swagger that he impressed upon the teens. John would also risk his life in the face of danger to insure the proper growth of the teens of Horner. For the team, Hen and John were a good mixture as their mentors. The fellas often hung together everywhere that they went. This was probably due to the fact that they played basketball and had been together since the kindergarten. Due to the intervention of Hen and John the fellas would no longer play for the BD leagues or allow them to gamble on them and win money that they never shared. Little did they know this would be the beginning of the rest of their lives."

25

Mike continued, "Skip and the fellas needed a metamorphosis in their lives if they were to survive Horner. Without the BD's dependency on their skill for money the status quo changed. The fellas were ready to be under their own protection. If Hen & John had anything to do with it, their training begins now and the basketball court will be used as the rite of passage for the young teens. The teens were to develop an adaptation to the new threat in the neighborhood. A Black Disciple (BD) with the high rank of Minister had arrived from prison with a new agenda. He would not rest until every able-bodied male from teen to senior in the neighborhood was BD. He also set his sights on females. The other urban societies (gangs) had once bore a verbal and social contract with the BDs through a shared history. These were the Black Souls, Black Gangsters, and the Gangster Disciples. The minister's name was Ram."

26

Mike went on, "He had appeared a hard bodied, beady eyed, dark figure as prison and murder had made him. He was feared and respected as an assassin in the days before he went to prison and had the same reputation in prison. Now he's back home with the slogan BD or Be Dead. This slogan equated to the blitzkrieg of Hitler, as Ram would rid the neighborhood of all possible threatening urban societies but BD. He was a success. I would visit the neighborhood after many of the other older members of the societies other than BD had disappeared, with one man standing as residue of the past presence of the GDs. His name was Little Ritty, brother to Knuckles, a well respected assassin that would rival Ram, since he ran the streets while he was in jail. Ram would later find that one of the greatest mistakes was leaving Ritty in the neighborhood at the request of Knuckles, who was more feared than Ram and was his hired enforcer for as long as he kept their contract. This is the outlook of the neighborhood that the fellas had to overcome.

"After Ram's victory it seemed that they had run out of enemies to fight. But next he set his sights on the fellas as strong, fearless, and a potential threat in the future. At the time the fellas were being trained by Hen and had gone under the name Black Panther Ball Players, named after the human/civil rights group. In this camp Hen would mold these men to be the best product that our neighborhood had to offer society and sports. Hen and John had worked day and night to groom men out of the fellas so they would not fall prey to the cycle of failure and death of Horner. In the name of the fellas' team, Ram had found a shady reason to approach them with malice. Black Panther Ball Players or BPBP:

These letters were similar to a historic rival of the BDs called the Black P Stones or BP or BPS. As Ram approached Hen and the fellas on the way to a game, with Knuckles, his enforcer, and about 24 henchmen, Hen did not flinch.

"Ram looked Hen in the eye as if he were an infant being told instructions from his parent and said, 'Y'all gone have to change y'all name.'

"Hen looked him in the eye like he had the FBI or something at his backside or some unseen force that he knew would protect them all and replied, 'Man, it's already a trade mark of ours!'

"Ram's henchmen jumped in between him and Hen with a 9mm gun at Hen's head and exclaimed, 'Muthafucka, don't nobody talk to our minister like that!'

"Ram placed his hand in between them, recalling the help that Hen had given to two of his sons while he was incarcerated, and removed the gun. 'Chill out! All y'all just chill the fuck out, I got this!'

"Hen, ready to give his life for what he believed in and for the fellas, stands with an even stronger stare as if no bullets would harm him and said, 'Y'all remember this was y'all when y'all were able to go wherever y'all wanted without worrying about getting stabbed or shot because of what gang you in. Y'all wanted then what they want now.'

"One of the BDs shouted, 'Man, shut the fuck up, we don't want to hear none of that Malcolm X shit!'

Ram left Hen with one thought. 'You got a pass this time, but if I see them uniforms at the Urban Fame tournament it's gone be something!'

"Hen, still without fear, said, 'Aiight.'

27

Mike continued his tale. "The entire time that this was going on, the fellas remained quiet with fear for their lives. That day they walked home with what seemed a 50% more effect of gravity on their faces than usual. That night they met about what they were going to do. Hooping was what they did and the ticket to their future! They weren't going to lose their futures for nobody. That meeting contained Bone, the youngest brother of Knuckles the BD enforcer. Knuckles had attended the meeting secretly because Ram had broken the contract by threatening the fellas, which contained his little brother Bone. Knuckles and Bone had another brother, Ritty, who would become the leader in change in the neighborhood and the largest opposition to Ram in the future.

That day the fellas decided the streets would become their basketball court and drugs would be their basketball as they would use them as a ticket to a better life economically, and guns as the new addition to their uniforms as they would need them for their survival against a much older, well established, and ruthless team as the BDs."

The First String

28

Khan listened as Mike went on, "At this time Horner was a collection of 14 buildings, with ten being 22-story high rises. Eight of the buildings were east of Hoyne St. and belonged to a different nation of organizations in a coalition entitled People, which were mainly Stones, Vice Lords, and Fours. There were six buildings on our end which were known as FOLKS territory, but all six were BD at the time, thanks to Ram's campaign of terror and takeover.

"In those FOLKS buildings where I grew up were two surviving GDs. One, by the name of Ritty, was always there from the time the BDs and GDs were in coalition as BGDs and the other one, Big K, came from Chicago's Southside where GDs had the highest population. There was one building in the FOLKS part of Horner that the BDs paid little attention to, as the parents had more control than all other buildings, 2215

West Lake St. This was the building where Skip, Bone, and the majority of the other basketball players my age lived.

"Natural to the fraternal bond of meeting another fellow GD, Ritty had aligned himself with Big K. Ritty gained K the acceptance of the residents of 2215 as one of their own. Though the BDs were skeptical of K's existence in the area, Ritty had put in enough work for them that his respect stretched further. The parents of the 2215 would call the police on BD activity every chance they got, for any crime. This made it impossible for the BDs to sell drugs out of 2215. Yet, the BDs didn't care, as they had five other buildings to make money off of. But such activities made the BDs resent the parents association of 2215, which they took out on the children of those parents who happened to be Skip, Satin, Hawk, Spud, Sconey, and the rest of the guys. They began to pick on the guys more and more as time went on. The BDs leadership resented the fact that such clean-cut students refused to join their ranks also. This kind of took the spotlight off of K and young Ritty, who were both the age of 21. There were others around that were 18 years of age and on their way to graduate from High School that were the older cool group of hoopers who had also not joined any gang in the area. These were the mentors slated for college. They took care of their mothers and grandmothers, along with siblings. Their names were Eric, DJ, Reggie, Du, Eddie, Owen, and Ace. Ace was

Satin's big brother and was the funniest guy in the neighborhood.

29

Listening to the story and noticing Mike's expression Khan saw a serene smile as a show of respect for those that he spoke of. He leaned in and asked Mike, "What was so important about these men?"

Mike returned, "Listen! You gotta wait, then you will see."

Khan, even more interested, sat back to listen again.

Mike continued, "The story comes together more as Ram and the BDs go on a rampage of recruiting to rid any potential threats. This set the environment for the greatest change in all of our lives, especially mine. For some reason Jay Bo the Co- Minister of the BDs, who also happened to live in 2215, noticed that the parents had nothing against Ritty and K. Seeing this, Jay Bo courted the two to sell drugs in the untouched 2215 building. Jay Bo would hire the two to sell his own personal drugs outside of the eyes of the other BD ranks. Being greater leaders, Ritty and K made Jay Bo another deal.

"K told Jay Bo, 'I know a connect on the south side that could give us all a sweet deal on a package. It will be close to nothing down cause he has so much and we could give you 30 percent of the take. Matter fact, you ain't got to put nothing down!'

"Seeing green, Jay Bo took the offer and gave them permission. What an idea. Ritty and K would start off with a two for $15 deal on dimes ($10 bags) of crack, which was a sweet deal to the area fiends (addicts), who usually got bad product which gave them a bad attitude. K and Ritty were not only business men but gentlemen that treated their customers with respect. They called their addicts customers or clients instead of fiends or hypes, as the BDs did. The users felt respected and the product was more potent.

"So naturally the BDs saw a decline in their sales but Jay Bo was receiving a growth in his, as well as Ritty and K. There was just not enough space for everyone to make money. There were not enough resources such as jobs that paid over $4.25 minimum wage that could be of real benefit to the impoverished and under-educated families in that caged project setting called Henry Horner after Chicago's former Governor so the guys felt that drugs were their only way. K and Ritty got so big that they needed new recruits. The 18 year olds (Killa) Reggie, Eric (G-man), Dj (El Diablo), Du, Owen (Big O), & E. Cool needed money to take care of their families.

Everyone in the projects were poor, so why wouldn't they? K and Ritty began to flaunt great wealth--they had new cars with the best looking 100 spoke rims on them. They wore the latest in sport fashion apparel and wore the biggest rope and herringbone chains that one could ever see. The older 18 year olds began to hang around them until one day they too started to drive up in cars and wearing the best clothes and biggest chains. Now the BDs are furious. Here they are on their territory, robbing and stealing to look better and survive, while these non-BDs were shining. Hell, naw! They weren't having that. The BDs had a meeting about it, in which it was brought up that they steal and rob K and his new crew.

"Jay Bo stuck up for them saying that it was his work as he called the drugs.

"The BDs asked, 'How come we as an organization don't benefit from it?'

"Jay explained that the parents wouldn't have them selling in their buildings but wouldn't bother their own family members. It was putting money into their families so they remained quiet. For a minute they left them alone because no one there outranked Jay Bo and they knew that he was stronger than them. What the BDs would do was to try to take every moment that they could to agitate and start a fight with K's crew; since they were outside of BD law, they were outside of BD protection. K, seeing and knowing this, made a decision to secretly take the 18 year olds to the south side to be initiated as GDs.

"Along with the new 18 year olds, he would take my former classmates--the 15 year olds and under. They wanted money to support their families, too, and wanted to be something different than the lower hygiene, stealing, robbing, and bullying-BDs. The basketball team made a decision behind their mentors Hen and Johnny's back that would move them to hurt.

30

"One day," Mike continued, "when the BDs came outside to agitate the youngsters of 2215 after losing a basketball game, they found themselves surrounded by 10 young men with their hats to the right which was a sign of FOLKS. The BDs had known that they didn't bring in any more members, so why were their hats to the right? K and Ritty walked up to the BDs and asked them if they had a problem with the guys. The older BDs said no and went to their building to get some other BDs to aid them in agitating the guys at 2215. Thirty BDs marched over to 2215 to be met by now 40 GD's.

"Pondering where they came from, the BDs called Jay Bo and alarmed him as to the now grown GD presence. Jay Bo went over to speak with K and Ritty on the matter. In private and away from the two large groups, Jay Bo and Quik represented the BDs while Ritty and K spoke for their group. Jay demanded K tell him the meaning of this outrage. K told him that they were now members of the GD Nation and under the laws and protection of such a society.

"Jay Bo seeing, this as a problem that would bring his leadership under question and possibly get him killed by the elder BD ranks, told K that he was through with the alliance and that he needed to leave.

"Ritty replied, 'You gone leave all this money Jay?'

"Placing money into Jay's hand, Ritty told him, 'We have doubled what we were making and here's your advance.'

"Jay couldn't believe it--his eyes widened. Jay began to walk away as the other BDs stared hard with ice-cold faces as they wanted to rumble with the 'intruders' of their territory. Jay commanded them, 'Well, come on, muthafuckas,' as he walked away.

"K and the guys kept selling their drugs and organizing their guys. Ritty asked the youngsters how they were going to protect themselves in the event of attack, as it was coming one day soon. He advised that he would never place a gun in their hands but knew someone that they could buy from, since they were making all of that money now. All of the guys agreed that they wanted to buy and two people were picked to ride with Ritty and K to get the guns for everybody. Skip and Reg represented both age groups.

"Shit hit the fan when Ritty started dating Jay's beautiful and full-bodied girl toy and the BDs found out. That only placed them in danger of Jay not keeping peace. The biggest thing that went wrong was Ram coming home from jail after serving a bid for conspiracy to buy drugs in California. He was home and had outranked Jay Bo.

"The first day back Ram was going to kill Jay Bo but decided he had further use for him. Infuriated, he asked Jay Bo how he let GDs that he personally ran out of Horner back into the area. 'You sold out our nation for money! It's BDs here who ain't eating, but these lil nappy head bastards getting fat?'"

31

Khan listened as Mike continued, "Ram slapped Jay Bo in front of every BD in the meeting of 140 BDs at a park near Horner. Jay's security pulled out their guns, to be met by the 50 men Ram was now in command of that had guns. It was clear who the ranking officer was in this meeting. After the meeting Ram met Jay in private, explaining that he had to slap him to show his strength and that others wanted to kill him but the humiliation was temporary enough for them to let Jay live a little longer. Ram explained to Jay that he needed to get rid of the GDs and put drugs from himself in the place of theirs. Either that or death was the choice of Jay Bo's. Jay, in fear of his life over those that supplied him money, devised a series of plans to rid Horner of the GDs. These plans involved BD ranks from the entire neighborhood, which included the immediate outskirts to the south of Horner, which was also BD territory. That added at least 73 more BDs to their count versus twelve members of the GDs on the 2215 count.

"The oldest was a 21 years old in 2215. It was a hot summer when the BDs set up a basketball game against the 2215 GD's out of the blue. The ballers placed a bet of $30,000 each toward the pot. During the game BDs began to come from everywhere, including the park and Rockwell BDs to participate in this friendly game for money. Having the area's best trained hoopers and the Dett Elementary champs for three years in a row on one team, 2215 aided them in winning all games. One of the BDs said that Du fouled him and that it wasn't properly called because they were cool with Hen, the mentor who happened to referee as a neutral agent that day. The BDs knew that the guys of 2215 who were mentees to Hen would not let them push

Hen around. The BDs told Knuckles to hit Hen and the others would follow, jumping him.

"Boom! A right came from nowhere and Hen was hit. Spud ran to help Hen and to block for him as other BDs began to hit him."

32

Mike leaned forward. "The BDs were all over 21 and largest in number, and they told Spud to get out of the way or he was breaking the peace treaty that they had in place. Spud refused and Ram looked over at Jay. It was the signal of a reason to rid the area of the GDs. The BDs swarmed the fighting teens from 2215, 59 against 10, as Ram pulled out a gun, along with others. Knuckles, the legend, shouted out, 'Not my brothers, not like this!

Ram lowered the gun in disappointment, as they had to respect Knuckles for what he had done for them in the past. He had saved Ram's life from Vice Lords that attempted to kill him. All the while, Hen was not the real target. Horner was quiet for days after, as no one from 2215 came outside. They had to let their broken bones heal. During that time the BDs began to sell out of 2215 as planned, while no one showed up.

" 'Cowards,' thought Ram and Jay as their plan actually worked. For one month the BDs actually thrived and began to build an empire of 2215 until--"

Knock! Knock! Knock! "Pizza is here," yelled an agent outside the door.

Kahn was awakened from his stupor of listening. Khan took the pizza to the table, along with the cups, and opened it as he poured pop for Mike. Khan looked with admiration to see a person survive such a horrid and violent environment in Horner, a place right here in America. He thought that things like this only happened in Third World countries between warlord factions. They sat and ate pizza quietly until Kahn asked, "Mike, how are you involved in all of this activity?"

Mike replied, "I wasn't."

Khan asked, "Well, how did you get to the murder scene?"

Chewing slowly on his last piece of pizza, as if to stall for time, Mike asked about his mother and stated that he wanted to share the pizza with her.

Agent Khan replied, "Sure, I'll get her," as he rose to pat Mike on the back, stating that he did a good job, on the way to getting his mother. As Ada approached, Khan congratulated her on having such a good son and told her that he

would be back, he needed to check on
something.

Collision of Bosses

33

Mr. G began to speak. "Looking back on the
things I learned from my family about our past, I
would say that it was a strange relationship. We
didn't quite get along with the Irish or Blacks,
according to my Pa. In the Village we would
keep to ourselves to preserve the way of the Old
Country. We often fought with the Micks—
excuse my language, Irish—" he looked at Dick,
"—over the business and for territory. We would
not allow them to come north. They held political
sway and power on Chicago's South side and we
needed a piece of the pie for ourselves. After the
draw of a few battles we ended up making the
agreement on territory as we mapped out the city.
North was us and the Jews, and some of the
South would remain to the Irish. As far as
business, bootlegging would be shared by all
three of us. That left the Blacks. We Village
residents were not quite the greatest enemy of the
Blacks as my Pa said." Glancing over at Law,
Mr. G stated, "They made a deal with your Pops
that if he and the others would stay out of the
bootlegging empire, the Outfit would stay out of
their numbers racket. They offered your Pops
protection from other smaller organized groups

like the athletic clubs as well as small jobs for his organization. Your father was very well respected to be a Black in those days."

Angrily Law replied, "You act like my Pops was proud of that. He worked hard as an employee, father, and community activist until the depression. You act as if he worked with your families because they threw him a bone or some scraps. He wasn't allowed into your Outfit because of race. His territories were too small to be significant to you due to racial boundaries upheld by the government through looking away from your activities. Yes, my father was a 'Policy King.' Like your father, he had to do what he had to do for his family and community's survival, even if it was illegal. What you fail to mention is how after Prohibition was reversed, your Outfit wanted in on the numbers racket that my father and his organization controlled. My father refused to give in, and your organizations bombed and shot many of his organization's heads to take over the racket. They pulled a sneak attack and the Jones gang had no warning. But they survived you and fought back. Yet all of that fighting left our neighborhood in an even worse condition than it was. The World Wars, 'Nam, and Korea saved them from your Outfit, as many of your members, along with my father's, went to protect our country. By the time that they came back either the FBI had broken up your Outfit or the rest of you that survived became shielded in politics. Politics was your new hustle, and again we were left out. Luckily as a war veteran my father and what was left of his gang could join the politics through the community block clubs and civil rights organizations that were still around and growing since they went off to war.

"Dick, your father and his Hamburgs took over the municipal government; Mr. G, your father and the rest of his people took over the unions and corporate entities. My father and his guys took over their blocks and the new trade that was left us, drugs. So how fair is that? Doesn't sound like our fathers worked together to me. It was the same up until now. Public housing was used to segregate our groups even further as only my people remain in them until this day. Though you changed the situation physically, Dick, the damage has been done innately and subconsciously. How are you going to regentrify years of dehumanization? Huh?"

Dick jumped in," So you want to point fingers at us as if we are racist and part of some large conspiracy! The joke is on you! "

"What are you talking about?"

"You forget that we are here by the threat of a common enemy that has attacked all of us and our families, past and present."

Sitting down again Law, Dick and G all seemed to put it together at the same time--the

FBI.

The Counter-Witness

34

On his way to check on the information gathered from the bull pen Agent Khan ran into a CPD officer from the tactical unit on the elevator. The officer was a neat and dark-haired Asian-Caucasian looking man. He was pretty young, with an innocent face.

Khan asked, "What brings you here to the Land of Oz?"

With a smile on his face the officer stated, "I guess the wicked witch of the west. I'm off to see the wizard by the name of Agent Khan."

Khan peered into his eyes and asked, "Do I know you?'

The officer returned, "What a coincidence. Agent Khan, my name is Officer George Mondo, badge number 536," as he extended his hand to him.

Agent Khan gripped his hand as the elevator door opened on the 24th floor, where he spent most of his time. The two got off the elevator as Mondo began to earnestly divulge that he had information about the murder that had happened in Horner recently. Khan asked him how he knew things when he couldn't get it out of the suspects and the only witness was in the office downstairs.

Mondo asked, "Can we go somewhere private?"

"Follow me," Khan replied.

Khan walked Mondo to an office around the corner from the bull pen, to enable a visit once they were done.

Inside the office, Mondo began to talk.

"I am a drug tactical, or tact, unit officer at the Wood St. Station, in which Horner is one of our main concerns. We have Criminal Informants --CIs--surveillance, and multiple round the clock undercover officers in that area, of which I am one. Though we don't have the murder on tape because it was not possible to get surveillance in that particular angle of the building, seeing that the Lake St. El train was constantly through the area and would block sound and the halls were too narrow to get a perfect picture. We do have camera snapshots, however. I have been on Horner for two years now with the job of taking down its drug bosses. Doing my job, I have seen unsolved murders there, constant shootouts, rapes--you name it. Things like our pictures and surveillance are unreliable. All we have to go off of is our CIs and the word on the street that we can catch. My concern here with you today is the kid that you brought in."

Khan returned quickly, to protect his witness, "What kid?"

Mondo said, "Look, I know that you want to protect your witness, but I was surveiling when I saw his mother bring him here--part of my job, ya know."

"This is federal business, officer, what business do you have with it?"

This is tact business as well, so I guess we share."

"What do you want to tell me about him?"

"I want to tell you what I'm sure he won't tell you: the facts about him and the direction that he may be going in."

Khan was wondering if the officer was just concerned with the life of the youth, so he would listen with the knowledge that everything isn't all that it seems.

Mondo said, "I noticed Michael and his brother Jim a year ago on my regular beat. They were clean-cut, well-dressed, and worked as youth mentors in the neighborhood. What they also did was sell drugs. Not in Horner, but as independents on its outskirts on the street of Warren Boulevard Boulevard. I would see these guys every day and wondered who they were and who they were with. It is not easy to sell near the territories of four different gangs without guns or support, but they did it. I noticed that Michael was out there every day earlier than his brother Jam.

"He had friends in the area, both male and female, but Jam seemed to ally himself more with the guys in 2215 as a friend. I could tell that Michael was smart, because he posted himself up a block from where he was with his brother, near two of his girlfriend's houses. This position was right on the border of the Vice Lord and Four Corner Hustler (4CH) coalition drug spot called 'double solid.' What was so strategic about his position was that he was in the center of BD, GD, 4CH, and Vice Lord trafficking which caused all of their clientele to have to cross his path. With concern I sent CIs to buy drugs from him. He was selling a different rate than those around him too. Whereas 2215 had 2 for $15, Mike would sell $5 nickel bags. It was easier for the addicts to get three for $15 or two for $10 instead of the one that the BDs, GDs, and Double Solid coalition gave them.

"I watched the young man because I feared for his life. Sooner or later the other older gang members would attack when they noticed a hole in their money. But this one was different from how he looked. He turned out to be more intelligent, stronger, and resourceful than I thought. I followed him and his older brother Jam as they got a ride home one day to find that they lived in K-town. Jam stayed in the house but Michael, he would stay out and hang with the neighborhood GDs. I saw Michael do their handshake with them and concluded that Michael was plugged; he was indeed a GD. He didn't seem to be into criminal activity and selling around K-town, which was to my surprise. I think that he wanted to be independent. Jam didn't show signs of being plugged, as they call it.

"When they began to go back to Warren Boulevard near Horner I got word from my CI that little Michael had gone to war with the Vice Lords across the street of the border, during which he put a gun to the head of their leader. I never saw that rage in the young man. They say he did it all by himself. He was bold. He then shot at one of the Four Corner Hustler Gang that came across the street and sold drugs on what he carved out as his block. He was claiming territory by himself, with no regard for his own life. This was an unusual feat for a 14 year old. He took the drugs from the 4CH member or four as they were called, who worked for the Solid Four and Vice Lord coalition, which brought heat down on him.

"After hearing this, Bone and some of the guys from 2215 came along with Jam to work the booming territory. They offered more drugs and soldiers and promised not to tell Ritty and the other ranking GDs if Michael would share the area. The coalition of Solid had trapped Michael by himself one day, asking him what was going on and ready to take him out when one of the ranking members noticed him as one of the Muslim community's members. Michael never backed down and they respected the heart and argument he made that the territory was open and their guys only wanted it because he got it going. He also made the argument that it was really BD territory and that he was sure the BDs didn't know that the Double Solid coalition were there. They all laughed at the heart of the 14 year old."

35

Mondo continued, "Following that, the guys from 2215 came into a coalition with Michael and Jam called Warren Boulevard GDs in which they were petitioning permission from the K-town GD headquarters to become sanctioned to be their own territory. Bone was to be the leader or Regional Coordinator, due to the optimistic plan that Ritty wouldn't go against his own brother; Skip was to be the Co-Regent due to his management skills and that he would provide the guns; Michael, the Area Coordinator (Spokesman or Chairman)--he took the territory and held great knowledge and debate skills; Big Man, the block coordinator due to his strength; and Jam the Chief Enforcer due to his strength and the fact that he was a top contending fighter in the neighborhood. No one in the group had won a fight against Jam.

"There were soldiers that joined Warren Boulevard street, like Joe, Hawk, T, Spud, Ric T, and more, which made Warren Boulevard street a formidable block of strength. Michael continued on not only removing the Solid coalition but the BDs as well. He gained a name for himself due to his forcefulness and bold traits that were a surprise to many but not to Big Man and Jam.

"One day an angered Ritty, along with what was left of his killers, came around to Warren Boulevard to seize the territory. Michael and all Warren Boulevard boys attended a meeting at the building in which Ritty appealed that Warren Boulevard was selling drugs that Bone stole from 2215 and that Warren Boulevard was indebted to him. Michael replied to Ritty that he brought his own product and owed him nothing. Take in mind that Ritty was always known as a killer--we never caught him, but we hear things. Then Ritty, who outranked them, tried to command them into his ranks, at which Michael told him, 'We from K-town and are under their protection, as GD headquarters outranks you' and turned to walk to the van that they rode in. While he was walking away, Ritty fired shots at them and all of them but one fled for cover, out of fear of getting hit. With smoke in the area, Ritty laughed as he figured that they feared his power to take lives. When the smoke cleared, one teen did not duck nor run and stood there staring, piercing into Ritty's eyes--it was Jam. Michael was astonished that their enforcer stood tall in the face of death.

"Jam then walked up to Ritty and pointed his finger to his face in anger and told him, 'You don't run us!'

Michael came and got his brother and walked him to the van before Ritty shot someone. Michael told Ritty that GD has laws against this and that he would be hearing from headquarters soon. Ritty knew that he wasn't bluffing and that they were K-town GDs because he had asked about them before they knew it. Called to a meting for his action, Ritty appealed to Warren Boulevard and then the GD board in K-town that they were too close to his territory and that he fought for the recognition of the GDs in the most hostile territory. The GDs granted Warren Boulevard to Ritty against the will of Michael and the others.

Transformation

36

Mondo sighed. "After a few months I noticed that I was surveilling two new members to 2215, Michael and Jam, and boy did things get more heated from there. Little Michael was the one that we documented as selling drugs the most. Little Michael was the one that we saw shooting more and more as it became addicting to him, and even natural. Soon he was running to BD territories to flush them out of places where they lived. Soon he was with assassination parties kicking in their doors. There are even stories where he worked for the $4.15 minimum wage in the Vice Lord building and had to cross BD territory to get his check from there at risk of his life. He felt that he worked hard for that check.

"He didn't need the money because he sold drugs constantly and was elevated to responsibility of distributing the drugs and lock keeper of the arsenal. The story goes that he grabbed his two guns, a .357 magnum and a snub-nosed 9mm, and walked through hostile BD territory at war time to get his check, which was like daring them to bother him. He was spotted by J.D. and R.P., who let out shots at him to warn the surrounding BDs in three buildings, two on his left and one and his right. They shot at Michael in the center of the path. Michael, as a 14 year old, wielded guns with enough power to force a full-grown adult back and fired toward both buildings with precision and ease, aiming correctly and not just shooting. Ritty and one of Michael's best friends, Joe, jumped in a car to go after Michael and aid him.

"By the time they reached Michael he had gotten his check from the building, untouched but as under heavy fire from the BDs in the south building. Michael put up a fierce fight in which our undercover tactical officers were in question to stop as they noticed that he ran out of bullets from his .357 six shooter magnum and his 7 shot nine millimeter until Joe leaped from the car and released an onslaught of gunshots toward the BDs for the life of his friend and brother Michael. Ritty then followed suit with Joe with tech nine shots from the passenger side of the car as he screamed an order to Michael to get in the car. He jumped in the car with Ritty and Joe and asked them to stop the car by the BD buildings. He and Joe, who had a semi-automatic tech nine, began to shoot at all of the buildings. When the firing stopped Michael exclaimed to the BDs that their members on the east end or 'low end' of the Horner buildings were on punishment and would never be able to leave their buildings. From then on, I guess Ritty saw his potential as a leader, because he moved up and up in rank and is slated for a good position. I know this because he is being groomed by Ritty's Co-Regent Sweets, who trains him day and night. The problem with that is that Sweets was trained as a Marine and now offers that training to Michael.

"This, Agent Khan, is the witness that you have. Make no mistake--he is cunning and very intelligent for his age."

Khan said evenly, "Hold fast. I have some things to take care of. Make yourself at home, officer."

He stormed down the hall to rush to the elevator in anger. He felt lied to by the sweet character of Mike. He was taken by the fact that he worked to help his family; that he worked in the community; that he graduated valedictorian; that he had good attendance in school.

In the meanwhile, Mondo had a devilish smile on his face, as if he had some sort of mischievous plan in the works...

Second Transformation

37

In the room with his mother, Michael tells her it will be all right, then the door flies open in haste. It's Khan. He takes a breath to calm himself and asks Ada, "Can you get your son to tell the whole truth?"

She says, "He usually does--why do you think he's lying?"

"I got my sources," Khan returned.

Michael, not sure as to what Khan thinks he knows, says, "What did I lie about?"

Khan retorted, "It's what you didn't tell me that is of concern to your character. What about the fact that you are a coordinator for the GDs? What about you shooting at BDs to get your paycheck? What about the fact that you hold drugs and guns, huh? To top all that, you are implicated in a struggle for power with the murder victim, Satin! Tell me about that! How does a valedictorian and community youth leader in training get into that?"

Michael's peaceful eyes turn a little cold with tears beginning to gather in his eyes as he looks up defensively at Khan. "You don't know what it's like to grow up poor in Horner! It is a trap! It's a requirement to be poor to stay in the projects and for some reason we are the poorest of the poor. You never let me finish telling you the horrors that we have to adapt to in that trap.

"We got out but the rest of the ghettoes were just as bad; the only difference was that the rent was higher and the territory was not as concentrated as the projects. In K-town the rent for a slum apartment was higher than the project apartment. Do you know the power of a Black woman like my mother? She's raising nine children on her own and has been since she was 13 years old, as she watched her mother die. A lonely 13 year old teenage mother that worked in a candy factory instead of going to school--she had only a fourth grade education. Men walked in and out of our lives and the end result was that she was stuck raising us the best she could, all by herself. She had no education to get a good job and not enough time to work, considering she had to raise all of us. She soon fell behind in rent in

K-town and we had to move to the North Lawndale neighborhood at the coordinates of Roosevelt & Kedzie. We had to face the fact that she was not educated in economic gain to survive outside the projects. My siblings and I figured that she was just not good with money. It wasn't her fault, I told them. She never had the proper help.

The tears began to succumb to gravity as a steady stream made a trail from his eyes, down his cheeks, and to the floor. Michael began to speak in a scratchy voice:

"Jam and I began a summer job under Mayor Daley's Summer Youth Job Training Program. The money that we received was still not enough income to dent the bills but it helped my mother and was an expression that we wanted to give her a break. We hurt that she never had rest in her life. The strength of this Black Woman was that she did not want us to go through what she had, having to work all of our childhood and missing out on the privileges and rights that are associated with the American dream. She refused to take our money from us after while and started to get her own.

"Jam and I decided to increase our income by taking our next check and buying drugs with it. I had mapped out that Warren Boulevard was open for the taking as I hung out there with my friends every day. I noticed that there was no real drug traffic within a two block radius. I had also noticed that all of the trafficking between three large drug distribution areas, Rockwell Gardens, Henry Horner and the row houses, had crossed paths at Warren Boulevard. This was a perfect spot and I gave thanks to my geography in Public Schools training for that. Jam and I got our checks and bought the drugs. We learned how to break them down from our drug addicted aunts and uncles, who also sold drugs. They didn't know that we used to watch them and that we were learning this family trade. Now we were in business, and my theory was right. Soon we needed an increase to our product, as clientele was building. We would go behind my mother's back and steal her bills to pay them at the payment centers. She didn't question what was happening and thought it to be a blessed mistake on the bill collector's part.

"One day my mother came running home and frantically asked us to come in and lock the door as she placed us behind the long couch and covered us up. She was breathing heavy and began crying.

" 'Mom, what happened?' asked Jam.

" 'They killed Frank.'

"Frank was a friend of one of my aunts that stayed in the neighborhood. Frank, my aunt, and my mother started hanging together heavily for a few months. We found out why. Frank, my mother, and my aunt used to sell a watered down version of crack to make money that they badly needed. They sold the drugs on someone else's territory because Frank thought it was okay, seeing that he was a retired founder of the gang that ran that territory. Frank was wrong and paid for it with his life. The gang leader that killed Frank came to admonish my mother and aunt, telling them to stay away from their property. The things women had to do to survive and care for their families were amazing and unbelievable.

"The next day I decided to tell my mother what we were doing. We used to always have talks, as I was her best friend in the family. She felt that I was smart and mature enough to handle adult conversation, as she started when I was 8 years of age. I walked up to her as she was crying and asked her what was wrong. She said that I was too young to understand. I placed my arm around her to hold her and told her to try me, I will learn. She did it and to her surprise I gave her advice back."

Curious, Khan asked, "What happened?"

"She said that my step-father had left her and that she didn't know how to take care of us. I told her that she took care of us before he came along. I told her that she was strong and beautiful as I rubbed her hair and held her hand. I told her that she had men that would never leave her as I reached into my pocket and gave her $250 dollars that I made hustling throughout the week. She hugged me and thanked me as she smiled. I walked away saying remember you can always talk to me, and this she did, time after time."

38

"Interesting," said Khan.

Mike continued, "So I told my mother that we were selling drugs and she told us that we didn't need to do that. She figured out who was paying off the bills and the fact that we provided our own transportation to school. I went to a school that was costly to attend because it was the number one school in academics at the time. Bus tokens were costly to a poor family like ours. Mommy asked us to stop and we did. After that the City cracked down on our landlord for code violations and labeled our apartment unfit for living. We had nowhere to move to and mommy lacked the credit to get a good place. We moved in with my older brother in a one-room shack. We were embarrassed to let our friends know that we lived there so we lied and told them that we still lived in K-town.

"The truth was that we lived right on the outskirts of Horner. Jam and I once again vowed that we would get out of there. The jobs weren't paying enough for the costly apartments in Chicago. The cost of living was so high. We'd rather die getting our hustle on than live like lames. The thug life ran through our veins, it was too late for us to change. We went back to the game. This time we would stay in it for the championship. Mommy needed help now! We needed help now! To Warren Boulevard we went. So, Agent Khan, I'm not the bad guy here as your source painted me out to be. I'm a kid trying to help his family to survive. A kid trying to help a great Black Woman that has survived a horrendous life of death, rape, and poverty get a break. I would rather do time in jail than watch her suffer any more. So I hustle!

"Under Director White, the Commons decided to pay for a hotel room for us to stay in until they could help my mother find adequate housing. They were so kind to us. They could have just let the State take us but saw that we were a working family unit and had an affinity for us, seeing that Jam and I worked hard, got straight A's , and aided in community programs, even when it was dangerous. The government grants to Commons were not enough and we had to move back to the shack. Jam and I weren't having that and we started to pay for the hotel. Yea, we would be in the game for a while now. But help came soon after. My mother received increased funds from the government after years of applying and Commons got us back into the projects. We were so happy but had no idea what it was like now. Here is what happened."

39

Mike's face grew grim as he explained, "The City Commons was the community center for the gangs in our side of Horner. It was led by Director White. This is where I received my leadership training and employment as a Youth. For a while I had been going to the Commons for work and recreation and noticed that the guys from 2215 had not come around for a month. There had been a full-out attack on the guys by the BDs that ended in the murder of one and the attempt on another. At this time I was from K-Town but stayed out of the affairs of Horner due to ignorance of the situation. I wasn't there for any of the activities of the BDs but this is what I was told happened.

"Ram and Jay Bo enacted a series of plans to take 2215 back. After the big fight at the basketball court which began the plan of take over by the BDs, the hand of the GDs were shown and the BDs now knew who they were and their leadership. This was all they needed to see, as they would gather information as to where each of them lived, worked, or where their family members lived and worked. They would harass them every chance they got to get them to change organizations.

"They tried it in a subtle way as they attempted to tell the youth that Ritty and K were using them and didn't care about them, or that they made all the money and BD would treat them better. The guys from building number 2215 or 15 as it was called knew better and would ignore such attempts, as they told Ritty and K about it. One of the old basketball teams starters, Cool, lived in the BD building and had began to stray away from the fold all of a sudden. Cool was a good friend to the guys in 15 and was known as a ladies' man alongside Skip. For two weeks Cool had suddenly disappeared as the BDs warned him that since he stayed in their building, the GDs would soon get him killed along with them.

"Seeing more and more money and respect coming in to the clean-cut youth of building 2215, the BDs got more and more angered. The parents respected the GDs, as their laws stated that it was mandatory that all members attend school every day, keep up good hygiene, respect women and elders, etc. The parents loved the fact that Ritty and K enforced these traits upon their children. Why not? It was the same thing that their fathers would have enforced if they were present or did not suffer from social illnesses such as alcoholism, drug usage, or other abuses.

"The same parents despised the BDs, who had laws that allowed them to exploit their youth and not add positivism to their lives. This was the final straw. Ram would enact his infamous BD or Be Dead campaign, as he did when they removed the GD threat before. Like any war leader, the first thing that he would do is take out the head of the organization. Usually K was seen washing his shiny 1990 drop top Ford Mustang. It was a metallic green wet paint job with green tinted windows and gold 100 spoke rims. In our neighborhood it was a head turner. K would shine this car every time that he got. This was his trophy and the BDs noted it."

40

"What happened?" asked Khan.

"One day at 5 a.m.," Mike replied, "K got a call that his car was on fire. Without thinking to call any of the other GDs, as there was a peace treaty installed that was the contract of the BDs that no war acts would happen as long as no one broke any of the rules set forth, K ran down the stairs to the open flame of his trophy. Running, it was his thought that this was the way that the BDs would break the treaty and was the beginning of hard times and war ahead. The BD leadership already had war on their minds, as one of the upcoming youth prepared a sawed off 12-gauge rifle for use. K ran to the car and was met by a sniper's bullet from afar that hit him in the chest. Seeing K still standing, the youth by the name of Quik had carried out his first murder as he ran nervously in K's direction. Quik stopped as he looked at the bleeding K and K returned a stare to the youth's eye. In a moment time stood still. The youth squeezed the trigger. No one knew what was happening, as the sniper's bullet was silent.

"Ritty woke up to a funny feeling that something was going on and began to put his clothes on and to load his gun as he called some of the other younger members--he was the oldest. While he was on the phone a loud bang was heard. Ritty and some of the others grabbed their guns to rush around to see what was going on. Their eyes were met with the flames of K's car and there was a bit of relief that the bang probably came from there. As they approached, though, melancholy fell upon them: there was a body on the ground, covered in blood, a figure shot in the chest with a hole where its head used to be. There were screams of agony as the alarm clock that day, the cries and pains of the friends of a dead man. After this there was a new beginning for 15. Defensive would turn to offensive. It was their turn to score on this concrete court in a game called life."

41

Mike took a breath and continued, "Having two generations of star basketball players would pay off for Ritty as he would become the head coach. Building 2215 enacted a plan that would affect the psyche of the youth for life. They would taste blood for this treachery. Everyone laid low for a month after the funeral. The BDs had their precious building, at the cost of a life. A fight for space as a temporary attachment to resources it was, indeed. One memorable morning happened out of nowhere. There were fires set in four different apartments on the outskirts of Horner. Along with that cars burned, as well. The sound of sirens came from all directions as the residents in the entire area were awakened at 5 a.m. There was what seemed to be an entire police station in the area, as well as firefighters and ambulances. When the smoke cleared there were five shot, three killed and cars aflame.

"What happened was that four of the BD drug houses had their doors kicked in at the same time as the inhabitants were robbed, beaten, and shot by the intruders. The cars of the leaders of the BDs were burned, and then the houses where they kept their drugs. The BD leaders Ram and Jay Bo received a call that they needed leave 2215 yesterday. The police were now gone to do their paperwork at the station as to these crimes. At noon Jay Bo received a knock on his door at his residency in 15. As his girlfriend was walking to answer the door it swung open fast and hit her. Four figures burst in like a tornado as two figures ran upstairs in her apartment, led by large automatic rifles. The other two went around downstairs to look around and secure the area. Jay Bo went to dash for his gun as he found himself at the end of a long black pole held by

Ritty. Jay Bo and his girlfriend were the victims of a kidnapping.

"Next, 13 figures dressed in Black were seen with guns in their hands as BDs were sent home as they tried to enter 15 to sell drugs, under the impression that the building was still theirs. All approaching BDs were met by gunfire. They ran to Ram to see what was happening and were warned by him to stay away until he could figure out how many were involved in this attack and who was attacking. There were only 10 teenagers present. There were no other GDs, as the thought may be. The GDs of the Southside wanted to come to avenge K earlier but were told at the funeral that Ritty had his own plans that included his guys only whom could handle things themselves. Ritty's thoughts were for personal reasons and the future. He had seen the GDs aid other territories like this and then they became indebted to the 'Mob' as it was often referred to. He would owe no tax to anyone.

"Looking at his team, Ritty saw championship potential. He gave them a speech to remember, as K was only a motivational tool after Ritty asked the guys if they wanted to see their mother robbed, sisters raped, be picked on, caused to drop out of school, to live in fear, then move away. 'If you want to see justice; come with me!' All I know is that after that Eric was nicknamed G-Man; Reggie- Killer; Eddie- Chino; Mandel - Do (short for Do or Die); Dj- El Diablo or Murder; Owen- Big-O; and Twan- Bone. Each man was elevated in rank and from then on showed signs of increased wealth. Building 2215 was theirs again, and they were home.

"After the attack the BDs called a meeting for a truce and dubbed 2215 a GD building by social contract. Jay Bo and his girlfriend were returned as a term of the truce. For a few months 15 flourished as the center of economic growth through the drug trade. By this time Skip and the others graduated grammar school and were freshmen in high school. They were open members in 2215. Ritty was either very brave or very stupid because he would go to visit his girlfriend that stayed in BD territory daily. Yet the treaty was honored and there were no shootings or fights between the two. Things had gotten back to as near normal as possible and the BDs were even buying product from Ritty, who was noted as having the better package. Ram resented the confidence on the face of the 22 and under aged group."

42

Sipping his soda–pop called pop in Chicago lingo, Mike went on, "Like clockwork Ritty was there in his car, which resembled K's former car but with a champagne colored paint job. Ritty waited in his car patiently as his pregnant girlfriend was due to come down stairs at any moment.

" 'What's up, Ritty?' Jay Bo began to converse with his business partner. Two other ranking BDs were seen in the rear view mirror approaching as Ritty turned to look at his mirror. Ritty turned back to ask Jay Bo as to the meaning of all of this company only to find a 9mm pointing at him at close range from the hand of Jay Bo. There was a flash as the gun went off. Lil Ed Jones walked up to Ritty from the passenger side and shot a tech nine at close range. Ritty was riddled with bullets as he lay in his car, barely moving, barely breathing.

"'Is he dead?' Ritty heard the last figure say as he saw him in the rear view mirror that his aching head was resting by. Out of fear of police or witness arrival, the BDs fled the scene, with Jay Bo and Lil Ed in front. As the last member of the hit squad lagged behind he took an attempt to insure that the job was finished and had ran back up to the car to let off one finishing round to Ritty's head at close range with a .357 magnum.

"Pow! "

43

Mike continued, "They say it echoed for miles. From there, Ritty lay in the hospital with 19 bullets inside his body. Amazingly, when his brother Knuckles and the others came to the hospital and asked him if he knew who did it, Ritty lifted his fingers with his last energy and made a sign. The sign was with the thumb pressing the pinky finger forming the number three. He then pressed the three to his chest with the same fingers as to his heart which was the sign of the BDs. As those around him attempted to decipher the signs, they ended up stating three BDs as an answer. Ritty signaled a slight yes as he passed out in the hospital bed with everyone waiting for him to die.

"For two months there was no hide nor hair of the members of 2215 as mothers sent their sons with relatives in fear for their lives. This time Ram was going to play it safe and would attempt to kill any member found. He even placed money rewards and rank out to any BD that killed or maimed a member of 15. After a few months I returned to work at the Commons in hopes that as a GD foreign to the area conflict, I would be all right. Ram and the other BDs stayed away from 2215 during that time in fear of retaliation and police investigation into that murder. They would not fall for the same set-up as last war with the GDs from 15, as security was placed on all BD stash houses. With no leader or direct contact to the other GD leaders, the remnants of 15 lay low and waited for instructions. They left their guns at 15, only to have them stolen by a former member that knew where the stash was—Lil George, who became a

BD. On the other hand, Knuckles had denounced his allegiance with BD, who had not only possibly been the death of his brother but were dishonest cowards and did not hold the policy of the peace treaty. They attacked an unarmed leader in the time of peace. Knuckles would trade BD in if only he could have his brother back."

Righteous Resurrection

44

Khan watched Mike's face closely as he continued, "At work now in the Commons, I stood in the gym watching the BDs, which included a one time GD member named Cool, all play basketball. I so missed my friends playing out there and doing what they loved and did best. Hen was the referee as the BDs played a hard game against each other in comfort that they ruled the neighborhood. With one minute left in the close game for the Commons championship the low end versus the high rise BDs were playing their heart out for the money that Ram was offering the winner.

"Light from the door behind me had spread as I was watching to see if there was going to be a winning dunk. I paid no attention to the door that opened behind me as I was watching the game. Wondering why I saw a ball bouncing by itself as all of the BDs stopped in mid-play, I turned to see what everybody was looking at. To my surprise the guys from 15 had arrived at the Commons on BD territory. *What does this mean?* I thought. As the crowd of the guys from 2215 spread, in their midst was a sight that was as if there was an instantaneous increase of gravity to the bottom lips and jaws of the BDs. In full view was Ritty on crutches--he had survived an onslaught of 19 shots at point-blank range with three of the world's most powerful hand guns.

"I felt a bit of pride--as GD still stood in Horner, so in the guys.

"Ritty, noticing the pause exclaimed, 'What y'all stop for? I got $10,000 on this game.'

"The BDs just kind of ended the game as they walked out of the gym to speak with their leadership on the matter. I admit I was scared that I would get caught in the crossfire if they were going to shoot. Accompanied by Knuckles and the entire new breed of guys from 15, along with the second string, they left the building. They had made their return known to the anger of the BDs.

As soon as Ritty was gone the BDs exclaimed, 'He had the audacity to come in here like he king or something!'

"I could only feel pride in GD and see the hate in BD. Hen must have felt my sentiments, as he only looked at me with a look that a change was going to come to the neighborhood. Ritty got on his crutches as he got out of the car at 15. He and the others went back and stood right in front of the building, as passing BDs were astonished at the face of what was thought to have been a dead man. They dubbed him Chief Half Dead, as he would joke with them, asking them to come over. 'I ain't gone kill you- yet. Send word to all BDs that 15 is back in play. If you want a job, come holler at me.'

"From those days on there were many battles to come. This is where we approach the murder of Satin."

45

Khan sighs as if to gather himself from the thoughts of the story that he had just heard. It was unbelievable that such things were going on in the projects. Teenagers that had to live like that-- there was not enough psycho-social data to diagnose the damages such as trauma, anger issues, and the development of emotional disorders that those who witness such horrors might have suffered. With that matter where were the proper conflict resolution tactics? These guys resolved their issues the only way that they knew how seeing that they have not been exposed to any other way. His eyes fell upon Mike in a motion of pity for the 15 year old. Khan asked, "If you were not there for all of that, then what made you enter the ranks? Was it the pride from the resilience of your friends?"

"No," Mike said. "It was the pain that the BDs caused me. Here is where I come in."

Recreation/ Wreck Creation

Mike resumed his tale. "After the eviction from Horner two years prior to that day, my family enjoyed living outside the projects where there were still shootings, crime, and gangs but it was less concentrated due to the houses and apartments of testament buildings being further apart. I had changed religious belief by then and had become a Hebrew, then an Islamic Hebrew in those two years. At this point in life I became industrious in learning, which came to a pause right after. I felt that I had exhausted myself and the things that I was learning so I attached myself into learning the new ritual in my life; throughout all of my learning was the brotherliness that I saw in the streets of Chicago Urban Society, the GDs. I was a disciple and had moved back into Horner which was predominately BD in all surroundings, north, south, east and west.

"The enemy to the BDs of Horner were the GDs under leadership of Lil Ritty. This would draw problems for me but could be avoided due to the BDs lack of knowledge I was GD. Plus, I was still respected as the neighborhood good guy and intellect. Yet my brothers and I had begun to re-establish our old bond with some 2215 G's and was given permission to set up a new area of GDs for the society with me as the Coordinator or

third in command and my brother as Chief
Enforcer. But we couldn't avoid the violence of
Horner forever and found out as my older brother
Jam and I walked home to 2245 which was the
building in Horner that we were relocated to
move back into, which happened to have become
the new headquarters for BD."

46

Mike pressed his hands against his eyes
briefly. "About four hours prior to walking home,
I had been having small feelings that tended to
increase by hourly increments. Jam had noticed
that I was not being my usual charismatic self out
there hustling on the blocks. Jam asked me what
was wrong and I told him that something ain't
right. I became nauseous from the irregular beat
of my heart, the constipating cramping of my
stomach, and the over powering anxiety that I
was feeling.

"After noticing the time passing and the fact
that I was not looking any better, Jam said, 'Let's
go home.'

" I immediately answered Jam saying, 'Let's
go to uncle's house today; something ain't right
about going home.'

" Jam, questioning my motives, said that he wasn't going all the way on the far side to uncle's when home was a couple blocks away.

"I said, 'But Jam, they at war and you know we saw Bone shoot Big Duck earlier.'

"Jam exclaimed, 'I'm tired of you trippin'! Ain't nothing gone happen to us; we been here for a year and they know we GDs but we don't participate in the affairs of 2215 G's. They ain't at war with K-Town G's yet and don't want to add to their troubles. Man come on I'm going home now.'

"Jam began to walk toward the building that we stayed in as I began to walk toward the bus stop en route to uncle's, when my best friend and fellow G Big Man grabbed my arm and stated that he believed my feelings that something bad was going to happen because he was witness that my feelings had saved our lives on more than one occasion. Big Man said that he knew that we had no guns with us but explained to me that my brother's chances are better with company. Big Man and I ran to catch up to Jam as I held my stomach running, blowing heavy breaths. The cramping got worse as we caught up to Jam and were approaching the building.

"The BDs were in sight as they would secure their building at posts during wartime, to be ready for their enemies and the authorities to try to capture or kill them. As we came toward the now one entrance, due to changes in housing, where the elevator was in the center of the building, then I noticed some strange activity in the BDs. It was then that I realized that the feelings that I had were because we were walking to our deaths. I knew that I had to buck up and stay alert if I was going to stay alive.

"We walked into the building as if nothing was wrong and we had seen no shootings, only to be met with questions by Snap, one of the most ferocious of BD assassins.

"He asked Jam, 'Aren't you a GD?'

"I looked around to see the positions and count the BDs surrounding us, looking for a chance to either escape or something to fight with if we had to. The only choice left was to fight or die, seeing that the entrances were blocked by a count of 21 visible BDs, all with guns. All armed with the mentality of anger from Big Duck being shot earlier by a GD. I blanked out at the moment of Jam answering the question of being a GD and found myself...

Michael's Inner Beast Released

47

"...Mustering all of my power into one right fist, I found it implanted into the face of Shaw, a feared BD leader. The next thing that I knew was that I saw my brother Jam with six BDs swinging at him and hitting him with pistols. As he was knocking them out one by one, he was overwhelmed. I felt pressure on my back and shoulders and blows to my face as about four BDs hit me. We were being jumped by 20 angry BDs with guns. After they overpowered Jam they threw him out of the gates into the mud, then grabbing me, which I refused to hit the ground to be stomped, they threw me out as well. Thinking that we were done for and to be shot I quickly went to get my brother off of the ground as the idea was to get away.

"The BDs hollered across to 15 which was only 30 feet away, 'Here go y'all brothers.'

"Thinking fast as to seem insignificant to 15 as to not be shot, I placed my brother's arm around my shoulder and walked the other way, away from both buildings as to show no allegiance to 15. We were not shot at by either party as we heard hollers from 15 asking if we were all right. We made a long trek to the bus stop with muddy clothes and swollen faces.

"That night we went to a GD set only 3 miles away on Jackson and California, where we met with K-town representatives and other GDs that had love for us Warren Boulevard boys. They were angered at the sight of our swollen faces and asked if we wanted them to go get the BDs.

We said yes and that we would make a plan but to our surprise a car with two ranking BDs was coming by.

"One of the folks stated, 'There go some BDs right there,' as Ant pulled out a .357 magnum and walked in the middle of the street to stop the car.

"Ant asked me if I wanted to shoot them for revenge. One of them got out the car and began to explain that he had nothing to do with our beating and disgrace and that he tried to stop it. His name was Prince and he was right. During the fight I heard Prince pleading with the BDs to leave us alone and telling them that we had nothing to do with the war.

"Feeling that all GDs are supposed to stand together anyway, the others pulled out their weapons as if they were going to shoot as I got in front of Prince to block for him.

"'A life for a life, we are even,' I told Prince.

"But the other one in the car aided in our beating. I went in the car and grabbed him and told him that he owed me one and that I will see them soon. I released them both to the rest of their lives. My religious teachings were that the life of a human being is priceless and that my pride and pain were only temporary."

"That night we went back to 15 to tell our story. Ritty asked us what we wanted to do as the GD headquarters called him and said that we had the choice to join 15. Ritty explained to us that this would not be the last time that they came at us.

'Look at you, your face is fucked up; I know your pride is hurt. You can't go home because it's either join them or die. If you join them we will treat you as one of them.'

"I replied, 'That's not an option- I'm a GD!'

"He said, "I'm a tell you like I told everyone else in this building--I won't put a gun in your hand, but the guns are here. If you ever want to protect yourself from menaces like those, if you want to protect your family from their ways, then they will tell you where the guns are.'

"That night I grabbed an M-16 and stayed on an open porch facing the BD building, on guard. If any of them came my way they would meet Mike G, my alter ego. From then on I stayed on security. I didn't drink or get high like the rest of them. I was an insomniac, so I was good for security and I genuinely cared for the bond of GD. I would guard them with my own life at stake. A friend of ours, Jane, had a house outside of Horner as she wanted to raise her family in a better environment. She still had a Horner unit in her name and out of respect for my brother and I being the nice, smart, hard working Gardners, she gave us her apartment. Now we needed money for that apartment and to help mom out. The drug money looked fast, easy, and plentiful. It was help now! We needed help now if we were to live to see tomorrow."

48

"I would become the greatest worker as my mathematics and intelligence paid off," Mike went on. "I moved up in rank as I was given control of the package for my hard work and dedication. I would work every day, every night, and every season. My fingers would curl up in the winter as I stayed out for hours on slow days to serve customers. I was kind to them, as I felt sorry for their plight. I was also grateful that I wasn't them. I did feel that I was taking down my community but what was a 14 year old to do? $4.25 an hour for part time was not enough. My family and I needed help now! The drug game was the only resource in the hood that was the help that we needed now!"

Khan brought up some things that Mondo told him that he heard about Mike. He wanted to get into the psyche of the witness to choose if he is a classic criminal mind in the making or if he adapted to an environment. He asked him, "Mike, what's this I hear about you provoking battles with the BDs? I heard that you were a leader now and that you seem to lack the fear of fire from their guns and of them. Your bold actions precede you. Enlighten me: what drives a boy of your stature to such measures?"

Mike takes a deep breath and says, "Honestly, you just get tired, frustrated, stuck in this small space in a circle that seems never-ending--it gets to you. You can't go too many places because rivals are all around. You got all of this money and get dressed up only to show the kids in school and the neighborhoods how sharp you are. The big thing was how I felt when holidays came. People in the projects seemed so stressed to provide holiday items that at most times we end up at war with the BDs because we exhaust more economic resources than they can. I couldn't be with my family for the holidays. I couldn't go home when I wanted to. I missed home. I have no youth now, I'm a grown a man at 14, paying bills for my family and myself. I don't have time to play or go on trips. I go to school but there I'm grown. Every day is a fight: a fight to be first in line to sell, a fight to get to school on time, and a fight to live. I had no rest! One day I snapped. I promised myself and the others that if I can't go home, the BDs can't either. We were going to conquer the building that my mom lived in. I started to not be afraid of death any more. I would go where I wanted, when I wanted. I'm reckless. I hate the BDs and their ways. They told my mother that they had bullets with my name written on them. The same thing happened to my little brothers. Michael Gardner is stronger than that. No longer will I be the threatened. I'm kicking ass and asking questions later. I can't live on the defensive. Don't want to be locked up in one space anymore. I need out! Out of the Trap!"

49

Khan noticed in Mike's psychosis that he was getting angrier and angrier thinking about what was happening. He saw that he was telling the truth and diagnosed him as a victim of his environment.

Khan interrupted," So I hear that you are the biggest upcoming threat to the BDs and that you are set up for leadership in GD."

"I ain't heard that, who keeps telling this shit about me?"

"Since you have been so straight with me I will tell you: an officer by the name of Mondo."

"What?! You gone listen to a dirty cop?! You need to ask some questions about him before you take his word as bond. Do some background on his dirty ass."

Khan would keep that in mind as he goes back to visit Mondo for a few more questions.

Khan turns back and asks Mike one last question "Did you see the face of Satin's killer? You are the only witness."

"I'm not sure. Do you have someone in mind?"

"We do, I will take you to the lineup in a minute; just let me stop to check on some acquaintances."

Agent versus Officer

50

Speeding up his pace as he rushed from the elevator, Khan rushed toward the office where he left Mondo. He wasn't there. Looking around now even more frantically, Khan looked into the only other place that Mondo could enter without clearance. There he found him in a break room, laughing with FBI agents as they traded stories about the way their day to day work place was. Raising his coffee-filled mug in hand, Mondo signaled a motion of alliance towards Khan.

"I need everybody to get out of this room," Kahn yelled, revealing his authority over the other agents that socialized with the strange visitor from the CPD. As they cleared the area, Khan asked, "What do you have against that kid? What did he ever do to you? Do you know what he has been through?"

Khan had cornered Mondo in the break room. Mondo showed no sign of fear or breakdown, as he felt that his place was right to counter the witness that he tracked on a daily basis. He said, "Let me ask you something, Khan. How do you know that the kid is not the killer? He is the only witness. How did you know that his own people didn't set him up? Did that ever cross your mind?"

Khan retorted, "I am a psychological analyst and interrogator of the highest class. I have been doing this for 20 years now as a career and have had it as an educational tool for 8 years. You can't tell me how to do my job, cop. I hear you're a dirty cop--is this true?"

Mondo laughed. "A gang member says I'm dirty and you, the great FBI agent, agree. Hmmm. Well, I guess that's why tactical are the ones that handle those little liars. We don't have the heart to listen to their lies."

Khan pressed on. "Has the kid or any of the gang members ever traded you guns for their members to stay out of jail? It is correct that you tact officers do hand in guns to gain vacation time and to keep your positions out of the uniform? It is also correct to state that you all get paid more and gain more hours also, right?"

Mondo shrugged. "Look, whether you like it or not, we are on the same team at some point.

We advocate and enforce for our system of government. It's not perfect, so how are we expected to be?"

Khan persisted, "You still never answered my question, which leads me to believe that there is some truth in what the kid says. I had you checked out. You are the leading tact officer on your team. You make the most arrests and have never gone under your quota for years. How is it that you sustain a greater record than even your partner, who trails you by many points? Is because they are Black that you torment them so? Why do you hate them?"

Mondo's face twisted in anger. "I'm not a racist! I may advocate for an unfair system that may seem to advocate policies that one race benefits from more than others, but I am not the racist here. I work every day more than 12 hours daily, sometimes around criminals like Mike. While they get away with murder and the degradation of their communities, I sit in cars, alleys, vacant apartments. It's me that sits with CIs that await another hit of the pipe. I watch those CIs place that pipe to their heads every day like a gun, and your precious witness supplies the drugs that are like bullets for that gun. You protect him?! All of those hours that I miss with my family to keep people safe that don't want to be safe--why? We ask the parents and leaders questions about the gangs but they give us nothing. I watch teens drive the fanciest cars, put on the fanciest clothes, and do the same for their kids or siblings. I watch my family struggle just to stay together. They have no father in the house because I gotta be out at work with someone else's kids! I get just enough to pay for everything after risking my life every day. I never once called them niggers. Who are you to judge me?"

Khan replied, "You tact officers are loose cannons. You report to your car every day rather than an office. You are detached from the uniformed cop for so long and have more freedom. Freedom like that can be intoxicating. It is power. No one is watching you. It's your word against theirs. So you take bribes and monies that your superiors don't see. You make deals that you feel are moral as to your unit without the consent of superiors. Why not? They aren't out there with their lives on the line. Anytime you walk up to those youngsters in plain clothes, you can be killed. You sit there slumming it so much that it sickens you as to how they have to live.

"What you don't know about me, Mondo, is that I did tact. I was that monster that you are becoming and at the point that I realized it, I quit. You can seek help for your growing sickness. You need sensitivity courses, Mr. Mondo. I will be recommending them to your boss. Get out of my face, Mr. Mondo."

As Mondo was leaving, he turned to Khan and said, "Maybe you're right-- but I wasn't always like this."

Walking away in the distance toward the elevator, Khan called out to Mondo, "Hey Mondo."

Mondo turns around. "Yes?"

"It's our job to gather info on every possible threat of terror to the people of the United States. Every organization--even yours. While you are watching them, be careful--you never know who's watching you!" Khan winked at Mondo as the elevator doors came to a close.

The Big Bang

51

Kahn got on the walkie-talkie and ordered some agents to remove the men in the bull pen into the lineup room and to prepare the way for the witness to enter the viewing room. Six agents went in to get the three most powerful men in Chicago out of the bull pen and into a room for a line up.

Law asked one of the agents where they were taking them. As they answered, "To a date with a woman named Destiny," one of them laughed.

Law replied, "That shit ain't funny, pig!"

The agent became quiet as seriousness and professional action became priority.

Khan enters the room where Mike was with his mother as he looks to the mother and says, "It's time."

Mike looked at his mother and nodded yes, as they would make a deal that would endanger their lives for some time to come. Mike walked down the hall, accompanied by Khan and two other agents, as slow as any man did who may be taking a march to a death sentence. Into an elevator that stood alone in the building they went in a direction to the line up room. The purpose of the secluded elevator was to keep the witnesses away from the possible path of the accused.

Dick, Law, and Mr. G found themselves stuffed in a narrow room with no chairs and bright lights looking forward into a large rectangular mirror.

"A lineup--they got us in a line up," Dick exclaimed with disappointment. Mr. G only popped the collar to his suit in confidence that whomever was behind that glass would never dare to finger him. The door swung open as two other men entered the room where Dick, Law, and G were being held.

There was a Latino named Flaco and a Jew named Merv whom were placed into the lineup as extras. Dick, Law, and G all looked stunned, as they all had business ties to the two. They could not believe the audacity of the FBI to place them all together. It was as if they were being set up to make one of them nervous enough to talk. *Was this really about the murders?* they thought. Flaco and Merv were connected in many ways.

Law got his guns from Flaco and his guys along, with his connect to his drugs. Merv served as a middleman between Flaco and his higher-up connects. Merv owned a few of the condos and office buildings that Mr. G used. Mr. G was the guy that Merv went to for Flaco's drug and gun supply bought in bulk. Merv moved the guns around with his trucking company, while Flaco supplied him with drivers that they could trust. The trucking company held contracts with the City of Chicago which were delivered to them by Dick.

Dick receives millions of campaign dollars from the League against Jewish Cultural Defamation, along with other Jewish foundations which one of Merv's cousins runs. There were a lot of connections in the room, but the actual focus was on a murder. An agent explained to the men that they were there as part of a lineup dealing with the murder of a 14 year old child of America in Horner homes. The men felt relief, as they thought that they were there for other clandestine endeavors that most likely wouldn't stick to them as usual. The relief was short, for in a narrow room as they were fit in, the bright and blinding lights were hot. Mr. G took off his suit jacket and held it in his hands as he tried to escape the heat. Dick loosened up his tie. The only thing that each man could see was his reflection. What a way to reflect on one's life.

52

On the other side of the mirror were Mike, Khan and three agents. They could see and hear the accused but the accused could not see or hear them.

Khan said, "Now get a good look at them first, Mike. We will let you hear the sound of their voices soon. Just take your time."

Glaring slowly from left to right, Mike looked at the men, beginning with Flaco on the end whom he recognized as the guy that they bought their guns from in Horner; Dick next to him; then his eyes got bigger as he recognized that the chairman of the board for the city's urban organizations, Law was there and next to him was Mr. G, whom Mike recognized from the news as having mob ties; next to him was Merv on the other end. These were some powerful men, Mike thought.

Khan stated, "Number one, step up."

Flaco moved up, with his piercing dark eyes and thick brows, as Mike said, "No, it's not him."

Khan yelled, "Step back, number one. Number two, step up"

Dick then came forward. Before Mike could speak, Dick yelled out, "Khan, did you tell whoever your witness is your hand in all of this?"

"Shut up, number two, your deceitful political talk won't work here."

Dick persisted, "Did you tell the witness about CoIntelPro?"

Mike looked up to see a frozen look on the ever–so-confident Khan. His face was as if Dick had struck a nerve.

Dick continued, "Do you want me to tell him? Let me tell you about your FBI friends, sir.

The FBI has affected the lives of each and every man in this lineup in a negative fashion. During the '60's they invented a program to gather information on all organizations that seemed disruptive to the U.S. government called the Counter Intelligence Program or CoIntelPro. After gathering such information the FBI then placed plants within each of these organizations, like bombs with timers. Like an explosion these organizations slowly crumbled, but the aftermath of the explosion was never cleaned up. Through CoIntelPro the FBI infiltrated local politics in Chicago, which affected my father and led to even my administration.

"With 'interest of the country' as their slogan, the FBI infiltrated politics that would affect the people's choices of the office of the president as the country's leaders. They would ensure that whoever was hired or voted on as our country's highest office would benefit the existence and continued existence of the FBI. The FBI needed a constant threat to exist to justify their existence. Political powers such as the mayor's office of Chicago, New York, or L.A. were very influential and powerful to the entire nation. A lot of financial business is done from these great urban centers and the FBI knows it. Powerful cities could deliver states and many votes to a certain candidate for president, and the FBI did whatever they could to ensure that the right boss for them is picked. My father and I were both coaxed by government organization under federal labels to deliver certain things such as laws with the promise of great federal assistance--you know, a favor for a favor. My pa promised Chicago to the Democratic candidate for Governor, who in turn promised Illinois to the Democratic nominee for President."

Law took over, "But organizations like ours put a stop to that. The Lords, Stones, and Disciples, along with the Black Panther party in

157

Chicago, had put a stop to such operations by the federal agencies. The people would not be intimidated. Through CoIntelPro the FBI attempted to turn the LSD coalition against the Panthers. They had plants within each organization to ensure that certain actions occurred that would cause war between us. Luckily we had much love and respect for the Panthers. Through reverends and ministers like those of the surrounding churches and Nation of Islam or Moorish Science Temples, we would have secret meetings to keep peace amongst our black organizations. We were all brothers of one common struggle. Each organization experienced racism in the '60's; each organization only existed for the upliftment of the people; each organization shared a common history which made our bind. Yet the FBI worked constantly to break that bond.

"Government powers at the local level saw our organizations as a political tool and a social healing to a problem that they faced and provided our orgs honors and monies through grants for our urban upliftment programs. There were streets named after orgs like Black Stone Avenue or Stony Island; there were parades that we attended; there were political banquets and inaugurations that our orgs were invited to. Then the FBI turned the state and city on our orgs and named us public enemy number one in our own towns. They turned on their once-honored citizens to the point that even near Horner on

Monroe Avenue, Fred Hampton and some of his members of the Black Panther Party were murdered by the CPD as representative of that municipality. This happened in other cities as well."

53

As the men spoke, young Mike listened to the words from the intercom. He heard sincerity in the voice of Law and the other man that spoke. Tears began to collect as the young 15 year old thought of the neighborhood landmark of the Black Panther headquarters that he passed on Monroe Street many times. As a youth the boys used to play in the abandoned house but had no real clue as to what happened in there.

Law continued, describing the massacre. "One by one, those Panthers were shot by the CPD, who were led by the FBI's information that they were a threat to this country and a direct enemy to the CPD. The CPD were not happy in Chicago until the head of the organization was cut off. Fred Hampton fell to bullets that Black and White in CPD uniform men alike hurled through blazing rods of steel because they thought that he had it in for them."

Dick jumped back into the conversation, stating that his father told him that his office received the information on the Panthers and the gangs. "He was told by the FBI that he lost the election and the Democrats lost their bid on the state due to the Panthers and the youth gangs. He said that the agent that reported to his office brought documents and pictures of Panthers and youth gangs at political rallies of important Republican figures. The agent reported that the Panthers were in bed with the Communists and that the Black Stone Rangers and the Main 21s associated with such enemies of the state as Muammar Ghadafi. They gave him supposed taped conversations between G, Laws predecessors, and those that they called terrorists and fascist.

"The truth of the matter was that my pa knew that these gangs were too small to be significant to entire nations and their leaders and that the civil rights movement was the most important issue to all blacks at that time. The thing was that they were shown to be a political threat to the Democratic machine and its political future in Chicago and throughout the state. So my pa declared war on the organizations that the FBI insisted were his enemies and the enemies to his life."

54

Mr. G stepped in to state, "Your race and organizations were not the only ones affected by deceit and mis-information through the FBI's CoIntelPro. My father and his family, along with their coalition, the Outfit, were also broken up through FBI deceit. Yeah, they did illegal things but when it came down to it, they showed love for America. In our rackets across the country we created jobs that many in this country benefited from. Whether it was the unions, casinos, construction companies, or bootlegging and numbers, we helped America out of a difficult position and asked for no grant money for it. In return, the FBI took our family affairs to the public and turned member against member by planting information that made it seemed as if certain members were going to snitch on the Outfit."

Khan interrupted, "You act as if your 'family' opened the doors for everybody! In Vegas the blacks that worked there daily, like Sammy Davis, Jr., were not allowed to enter the front door of your establishments. They had to go out the back door after entertaining your people and go over to West Vegas to hang out with the other blacks and Native Americans. Then you Dick-- how many contracts have your people handed to the black population? And you said it yourself, your father's CPD were the ones that attacked the organizations, not the FBI. Law, how much of your drugs have made a positive influence on your people? It is you bringing the money to drug lords for their product, not the FBI."

Flaco and Merv just stood there, looking as if they wanted to draw no attention to themselves, but they had a few things that they wanted to add as well on the actions of the FBI on their people. They remained quiet, as there was no need for concern since the focus was not on them. They would have their chance to speak soon enough.

Dick, Law, and Mr. G began to shoot back words at Khan simultaneously.

"Language and information are power and you FBI used it to manipulate us all and you are using it to manipulate your witness." Dick took over the conversation as he seemed to be the spokesman. "It was you who took the positivism and leadership away from neighborhoods like Horner. What would have happened if you had never removed leaders like Martin Luther King, Elijah Muhammad, Malcolm X, Noble Drew Ali, Chief Malik, Chief Bull, Larry Bernard Hoover, Fred Hampton Jr., David Barksdale--the list goes on. Your agency has files on all of those leaders. Your agency provided the information that got each one of them either murdered, imprisoned, ostracized, defamed, or exiled. Had you not had a hand in it, who is to say that the neighborhoods would not be different? Who's to say that all of our people's relationships would not have improved in this great melting pot that we call America, our home! Huh? Who's to say? And who is to say that one of your agents did not pull the trigger on that young man in Horner?"

Mike yelled out, "Satin--his name is Satin! Remember him. He had a name. He was a child like me and could have been a doctor or something, who knows?"

55

Kahn yelled out, "Silence! Just shut up, all of you in that room. Now Mike, tell us," he paused, "do you recognize any one of them as the killer of your fallen brother?

Mike looked over each one of them carefully as the scene came to his vision as a memory. He traced each moment: The children coming through the door; the laughing and loud conversation; the happiness to get to parents that were missed; the gunman rising from the midst of those children; the dark figure in a hooded sweater and wig; the flashes from the gun; with resistance the face of the dark figure of the killer began to develop. Mike turned to Khan to answer him with a look of great fear in his large round brown eyes. "I know who did it," he said, shaking.

A tear began to slowly crawl down Mike's cheek as his face slowly crept up from a darkness to meet agent Khan's eyes. He signaled for Khan to come closer as Khan bent down to meet his mouth with an eager ear. The boy now spoke with a look of anguish upon his face; his mouth moved slowly and heavily as if gravity had increased on his lips only.

Khan rose slowly, with his back facing the reversible mirror and stood still in place with a look of disbelief. Khan went through his entire thoughts, as all of his college years of psychology had not prepared him for what he had heard. In college Khan was taught that it was usual to look at the individual to commit crime but not this. A collective of individuals to commit such heinous crimes was unusual. Maybe *Michael Foucault and Roberto Freire were right*, Khan asked himself in a low tone, as if his throat was thick with a dry substance, that the line-up be freed at once. A bell rang and the door to the chamber was opened.

"You are free to go!"

Upon exiting Dick, Law, Mr. G, and even Flaco and Merv all began to put up a fight with the guards that protected the door to the witness and Agent Khan. There was a great struggle but Law was a man of great strength, as he seemed to get all over the place knocking out agents with his boxing skills that he earned from the park district. Flaco and Dick were great wrestlers, as was noticed when the agents were flying through the air, only to land on solid marble floor. Mr. G didn't waste time fighting, as the slender man snaked his way around the commotion.

An agent yelled, "FREEZE!" and the men all paused at the sight of the gun in his hand. They had penetrated the other side and laid eyes on the witness at this point.

Law began to speak. "You held us against our wills all of this time and gone just tell us to leave as if nuthin' happened. You know how much money I missed?

"I'm in papers, missed dinner, time with my family and you gonna just send me off with no explanation?" added Dick

"Somebody better tell us something!" they all found themselves saying collectively.

"Lower your weapons!" Khan ordered the agents to lower their weapons with the intentions of sharing who the murderers were. At least he could give them that much, he thought.

Both Khan and Mike turn to face the men that were in the line-up and began to whisper to them.

There was an immediate uproar as Law shouted out "Hell, naw!"

Mr. G stated, "I don't believe this shit!"

The others were as quiet as a mute, with a look of great awe upon their faces.

Dick began to speak. "You mean the murderers were here the entire time and you let them go? The great inspector Khan duped by those that he trusted most."

One of the agents in the room asked Khan if it was the crooked cop that they had put out of the building and the other agents thought, *Yeah, it was him and his cronies.* They began to scramble to get a team together to go out and get him.

"Halt!" Khan stated to the room, "No, it wasn't him. The murderer had been watching us the entire time. The murderer planned this from the beginning, even before the murder was committed. The murderer picked up the phone and called each one of our offices. It was the murderer that has been watching us the whole time, knowing that to place such men as ourselves together would only lead to the greatest confusion, as none of our organizations were innocent--not even the witness. We would have been so deep in shit that this case would have never been solved, as many like it have been through the years. These murderers have descended from organizations that have spanned centuries and have gone unknown getting away with murder."

"I can't take this; who the hell was it?" shouted out Flaco. "My nerves--I have a panic disorder!"

"You of all people can see the truth. All of you are involved in this great melting pot of races and cultures. Can't you see who did it?" Then the suspects simultaneously began to look up and out into the expanse beyond the room as they all simultaneously ran from the building, but it was too late. They all ended up on the sidewalk outside the federal building, looking in one direction in great awe and disappointment. Agent Khan looked up and sighed as he remembered a great lesson from a quote and said, " 'Is it because of laws that crime exists or because of crime that law exists?' Michael Foucault, *Body of the Condemned.*"

Michael replied to the quote, "Where there is a lack of resources, there is an abundance of crime. Michael Gardner from experience."

The End

or New Beginning.

What Michael told agent Khan was that he remembered a ring on the shooter the morning that Satin was shot. When he and Khan saw the ring again it was on the fingers of two people that were in the F.B.I headquarters that day, the dirty cop officer Mondo and F.B.I agent Pride.

Khan to all agents- 'Pride is to be found and detained for questioning in the murder of 14 year old Satin Harrington. Agent Pride along with Mondo has been identified as bearing a symbol seen on the murder scene on their pinky fingers. It is a ring bearing a Compass placed atop a square with a Capital letter G in the middle'.

They couldn't believe it! The F.B.I was once again locked into an investigation with the famed Freemasons. The F.B.I had investigated the organization before as a possible subversive movement during CointelPro in the 1960's. Information had come up that many of the leaders of the Civil Rights movement as well as the Black Panthers were members of the Freemasons. Along with the Black leaders there was a finding that the Freemasons were leaders in other organizations that the F.B.I investigated such as the Ku Klux Klan, the Mormons, and the Baptist Church. It was also found that most of the leaders of the U.S. government were in this organization such as the greater percentage of U.S presidents, senators, and other high offices which included the F.B.I.

Such connections were found to have come in handy in world famous cover-ups of murder such as the Jack the Ripper serial killings in England and the death of former Freemason Captain Morgan in America. The record of historical Law on the

Captain Morgan murder stated that the evidence was covered up by the sheriff as well as judges whom were later convicted by a citizens board that later became the third largest party system in the U.S besides the Democrats & Republicans—The Anti-Masonic Party. Other findings of Freemasons and murder accusations that were covered up are the Lincoln assassination which occurred in a theater owned by Freemasons and was carried out by a John Wilkes Boothe (a documented member of the Freemasons). James Earl Raye was also a documented Freemason from the southern jurisdiction whose members founded the Ku Klux Klan based upon knowledge from the ancient secret organization. The F.B.I findings on the organization were also under review by the CIA due to international unsolved murders which involved members of the Freemasonic society. The investigation came to an abrupt halt when it was closed by the office of the President and secretary of State in the 1070's stating only this:

the Freemasonic Organization is found to be an honorable organization with high patriotic support for the United States of America. Though some members have been found to have been charged in murder cases throughout U.S. history the evidence is highly inaccurate and inconclusive that the organization had planned assassinations that equate to serial murders throughout the world. The numbers of individual members whose names have appeared in murder investigations are too small in number to reflect an organization of millions

*throughout the world. With this in mind the F.B.I is
closing all cases and investigations on the
Freemasonic institution for good.*

Khan's heart could not believe the information that
he received in the folder that he had asked one of
his agents to retrieve. Seeing that it was possible
that the hundreds of annual murders of children
could have been enacted from such a connected
organization as assassins for hire, Khan wanted to
reopen all investigations on the organization.

*This would have to go directly to the F.B.I's district
chief,* thought Khan.

With high adrenaline and deep breaths Agent Khan
storms into the office of the District Chief of the
F.B.I with the files on the Freemasons as well as
officer Mondo & Agent Pride. Along with those
files Khan provided separate pictures of the two
with the ring emblems of the Freemasonic Order.

"Chief, it is of the most urgent matter that we
assemble an undercover investigation of these two
officers of the law and a possible connection to the
Freemasonic organization as possible assassins for
hire!"

The Chief replies in a fire of rage, "Khan as one of
my top agents and investigators you can not
seriously tell me that you have enough evidence to
bring this matter up! If I allowed such an action the
both of our careers would be over!"

"Sir, I have an eye witness that can tie the case together,"

"Just stop it Khan! There is no 15 year old witness that can lead to an investigation that will drag the name of the CPD and F.B.I down and make our country look dishonorable in the eyes of the world. You are to cease all activities in this case immediately! You are off this case Khan. Agent Pride will head the closing of this investigation. I am ordering the release of your witness as well as clearing Agent Pride and officer Mondo of all accusations!"

"Sir with all due respect we have uncovered so many leads on high end crime throughout this investigation. We have the corruption of the Mayor of the City in connection with a mobster, a gang leader, an arms dealer, and a crooked real estate mogul. We can change this City and send it off to a better direction! Along with that we can heal this City of its pain as the murder rate can drop due to the exposure of mass murderers and the crooked empire of the government. You can't …"

"Damn it Khan I can and I will! I have spoken and you will respect my command!"

"Why are you so against helping the people of Chicago and the cities of the world whom suffer so much?!"

Somberly the Chief begin to educate agent Khan, "Khan you have taken down corruption from all sectors of government to make this country a better place and our democracy a great example to the world. Because of that and your clearance I now see the need to let you in on an on going investigation that the national office has us in on in coalition with the office of Homeland Security and the CIA."

The District Chief takes a key out of the inside pocket of his wool blazer and begins to unlock a cabinet within his office. He then pulls out a file and hands it to Khan. Khan opens the file and begins to skim through the information as his eyes begin to bulge at the sight of pictures of F.B.I informants both criminal and part of State government.

Khan looks up at The Chief in surprise,

"You mean our office knew that Mayor Dick D, Mr. John G, Jr., Merv Goldstein, Antonio 'Flaco' Diaz, Lawrence Malik Jones, and Anthony 'Lil Ritty" Washington was all working together?"

"We had them in on the very same charges that you brought them in on but we made deals with them that were in the best interest of the bureau, the city, and our nation. What I'm saying Khan is that they all work for the F.B.I and have been for years."

"I don't understand! Why are we working with the likes of these criminals?"

"Khan you were smart enough to catch what took us years to uncover in a matter of days. Like all operations they are bait to catch a fraternity of assassins whom are behind the murders of youth and adults across our nation and have been since the beginning of our nation."

"The Freemasons?"

"No, there is an organization of individuals much more powerful than even the Freemasons, much more subversive. We became knowledgeable of their existence when the Freemasons brought it to us during the investigation on them in CointelPro. Many of our agents whom had gotten close to the organization have either disappeared or had resigned the Bureau due to fear or stress. We don't know the name of the organization but we found that we needed some powerful people on our team if we wanted to catch this organization of assassins. We are close to them Khan. I need you to head this team along with others to stop this organization. For some reason someone wants the youth of Chicago dead. We don't know if it is for the value of the property that the youth organizations and their families occupy, an ethnic cleansing campaign, or anything but we suspect that this fraternity is assassinating America's youth in impoverished Black neighborhoods now. The 6 men are cooperating because the organization has at periods in time affected each of their races throughout the city leading campaigns of murder and mayhem that has recreated history in a direction that the races never really planned. The interest of this organization seems to be money and the control of the United States as a government and a people. They will stop at nothing so you should stop at nothing. You are ready Khan. "

Agent Khan left the room with a queasy feeling and told the Chief,

"I will get back to you with my answer sir."

As Khan leaves the District Chief's office he views the ring on the chief's finger- *Chief a Freemason?*

To Be Continued

Author's notes

  Right now the spot light of the world is on
Chicago, IL. When you turn on the local and
national news you will see the national and local
spotlight on our city for two reasons; the First is
our resident president Barack Obama. Everyday
he went from a local headline made from
Chicago to a national platform as our local hero
announced his candidacy for the U.S. presidency.
The next thing that you see our city on the
national news for is our Crime rate. Again,
Chicago has captured the media attention when
Actress/ entertainer Jennifer Hudson's Chicago
based family was found murdered. This heinous
crime included two adults and a seven year old.
Weeks later another bright star, R. Kelly had a
nephew of his killed I Chicago. In the same week
two teens were found dead in Englewood
neighborhood of Chicago. The news has reported
over 400 reported shootings of children by
violence in Chicago in 2008, which is not to
mention the adults. We are losing our futures to
violence! There are so many ways to die but in
our city violence is the popular one amongst the
African- American population. You hear that,
American. This is an American problem that is
rampant amongst its poor but happens
everywhere. We have many young children
murdered everyday; some of our police that serve
and protect us partake in the murder of our youth
as well. But there are noteworthy officers that
actually care about our plight and go above and

beyond the call of duty with their lives on the line to lend a hand to our communities.

We have put in place many note worthy programs and campaigns such as the gun turn-ins and community organization involvement. These programs are successful but are not enough. Yet, without such aforementioned programs I'm afraid that there would be even more found dead due to murder and violence. This book appeals to the rationale, compassion, and humanity of the American reader to help slow the violent deaths beginning with Chicago going through every city of the United States and then the world. This book appeals to the American people through asking Chicago communities and community organizers to stand up and stand out against the way people in this city are living.

We now have an outsider, Jody Weiss, as Chicago's new Chief of police on news stations and in newspapers in Chicago speaking of gathering a police force of 400 cops to go after gangs as the perpetrators of the majority of these deaths. The fact is that Jody is a former Federal agent that was appointed to the position of Chief of Police that even the CPD officers don't feel that he deserves. The fact is that Weiss has never worked on Chicago's streets yet, alone grew up here. But let us focus on the larger facts. Weiss was an F.B.I agent correct? When you look at the history of police involvement in Chicago *Street gangs* there was a recent F.B.I and CPD coalition that took out the leaders of nearly every *street gang* throughout the city. As a former member of one of those gangs I found that the people that we thought lead us were not in charge! Our true leaders were the F.B.I / CPD coalition.

The truth is that many leaders throughout Chicago's city street organization at one point in time were F.B.I informants! If you are shocked ask the higher members that survived. The F.B.I made their cases against the likes of Larry Hoover, Jeff Fort, the Vicelords, Four Corner Hustler, Latin Kings, Spanish Disciples, and more through criminal informants that were in leadership positions in these organizations. I take no political stand against law enforcement but I stand with the people of the city when I bring up the fact that those involved in taking down the gangs could have coached their informants whom were in powerful leadership positions to redirect the energies of the gangs which were community organizations that the government once supported in a more positive direction. Law enforcement only seemed interested in getting the informants to continue negativity in order to make a case on other leaders and disband the organizations. The coalitions on street gangs were successful in their endeavors to take out all of the major gang leaders. So why are the media of today being told that the same gangs are the ones perpetrating these violent crimes? Shouldn't Weiss know that the heads of every Chicago *street organization* have been cut off since the F.B.I was involved? Now you have warlords on the Cities Streets with no leadership. Isn't this the same thing that governments that invade other countries do when they cut off the current leadership? There is always misled violence when there are no leaders to control things. Just look at the news around the world were large organizations of headless nations, political groups, religious factions, etc, are and you will see the same cycle of violence that plagues the United States of America with emphasis on Chicago. I am calling for peace!

Yet, I never speak on problems without the presentation of some sort of solution. Here are some solutions that Mr. Weiss and the community can develop and progress that may help put our city in a better place:

1- **Support programs that constantly study and treat Chicago's violent areas such as the UIC Chicago Project's Cease Fire.** Keep the funding coming to such a successful program because they actually have documented proof that they work in neighborhoods that they are active in. Violence is down in all Cease Fire zones. Jody Weiss needs to listen to a panel of youth led by community leaders along with professionals such as Cease Fire when dealing with the violence in the city.

2- **Institute the Exodus or Exit Us Program** at community schools. What this program will do is have adults that are retired or do not work to hang out around schools with video cameras and picture cameras ready for criminal activity of any kind rather its doe by citizens or the authorities. Such an action will slow crime around schools just as the city has all of the expensive cameras in neighborhoods of high crime. Citizens can also get into their windows if they live around and near schools before children attended and when school lets out. Along with that we can obtain funding to hire out of work veterans as a security force to protect our children as a valuable resource. Of course these security officers will pass a background check as well as mental examination before hire. Our honorably discharged soldiers are trained in conflict resolution and may have resolved issues with groups during war without any violent conflict and can do the same for our children. So, exodus gets the community involved as well as provides jobs for our discharged soldiers where employment is hard and their skills are wasted.

3- **Economic Education Programs-** educate communities on wealth building and the vocabulary of wealth. Along wit that aid those in crime ridden neighborhoods to recognize resources that build wealth and provide the tools for them to utilize the knowledge of wealth in a work plan that will ensure that their children inherit wealth and will not have to participate in criminal activity due to lack of resources. Such a program can be backed by banks, insurance companies, investment companies, etc. I'm sure that they will all be happy to aid in such an endeavor as the services will return those that they help to them as clients.

4- **REINSTITUTE RITE OF PASSAGE PROGRAMS FOR TEENS THROUGHOUT IMPOVERISHED NEIGHBORHOODS.** If we bring mentorship through fraternal programs back to our communities such as those in Africa, Australia, and other world communities that partake in rites of passage, what would be the need for gangs that are disenfranchised from their communities? An American community needs to be built and our people strengthened as one people of one country. Maybe this can be a reality with the example of the Obama administration.

5- **TRUE REFORM FOR FELONS-** We need to back programs that are truly aimed at reforming those that break our laws and not punishing them both when they go to our governments or corporation jails and when they come out. We need to support the efforts of Danny Davis, Dorothy Brown, and others as they fight for legislation that will allow felons of all races (that have not been convicted of crimes such as rape, theft, and crime but sold illegal drugs to survive) to participate in the American dream and to be allowed to work a job. To allow felons to attend college in which they can not do under the current law. The same felons are returned to our streets with no hope of a job, no counseling for being taken from open society and no real counseling for being reintroduced into general society. Such felons become repeat offenders because they have no resources and often see only one option of returning to what they know to survive over just dying.

6- **The Community Police Program**- This is a program that takes community members of the age of 21 and up and aiding them to become police officers that will live in the community that they grew up in and are a part of. A citizens board or community organization along with the alderman, neighborhood police precinct, community colleges and Universities, will partner to take 10 worthy and qualified community citizens in a common ward and place them through a college criminal justice program, provide some funding from the state or from private grants to pay for tuition. The police training academy and the stations of the ward would provide officers with the best record of community connections and service to mentor the student along the road of becoming a police officer for the ward or community from the beginning, through the academy training, and afterwards. Once these students become officers the City should take over and provide housing in the community for those officers to live and work from. Along with that the city should also acquire properties in the neighborhoods that will act as beat stops in which officers can constantly park their cars, get out, hang amongst the community and mingle, keep warm, eat lunch, etc. A fresh class of 10 Community Grown police officers should be launched every two or four years to keep the connection between the community and police officers growing strong. The reason that this program is being proposed in that if you look at the neighborhoods of Chicago's borders and Bridgeport where there is a high presence of police families, the crime stats are the lowest. Along with that police brutality is also low as the families know and love the officers and the officers have a cultural bond to the community in which they stay. Growing up in Horner we were brutalized, dehumanized, and harassed by officers that did not understand our way of life. These officers had no regard for us as citizens and felt that we should not be free in this great American society. This lead to the character of Mondo whom is a real officer that tainted my life as well as many young lives in Horner, Rockwell, and Cabrini Green. If you were to ask elder Blacks from Bronzeville about the days where the Black cops were only allowed to work Black neighborhoods, they would tell you of the bond that they had with those officers. They would tell you of how they all knew each others families or how they brought them lunch and coffee, or how those officers were heroes. Let us go back to that and save our neighborhoods. Communities, please push come Aldermen, Senators, and Congressman to participate in giving you police representatives that will serve and protect your community and its interests!

There is much more that I can suggest but I will save that for seminars and works with the people.

THE CALLING

We are looking for stories of under privileged youth from the ages of 12 to 32 years whom currently live in violent neighborhoods to place into a book as well as on television programs that will work with us. We need to know what neighborhood you are from such as Englewood, what violent things are happening, why you feel the violence is happening, what you think can be done to stop it. We are also seeking those that participate in violence and would like to hear from you as to why you and your partners (if any) are at odds with an enemy. (NAMES & IDENTITIES WILL BE KEPT ANONYMOUS UNDER THE PROTECTION OF PSYCOLOGISTS, SOCIOLOGISTS, & SOCIAL WORKERS. NO LEGAL AUTHORITIES WILL BE CONSULTED ON ANY MATTERS FOR ANY CIRCUMSTANCES).

We are also looking for College graduates that come from the very same dysfunctional families that those whom perpetuate the violence on our city streets come out of. We are looking for former members of Street Organizations (those whom were actually active and on count, paid dues, and went to meetings from 1985 until 1995), community organizations, counselors, Licensed Clinical Social Workers, Psychologists, Mentors, and all that want to volunteer whom are from low- income backgrounds and have survived to have gone to college and now work in such professions.

Many of our youth and adults on the street suffer from trauma due to violence in our city. This trauma usually goes untreated and the perpetrators and victims often become heartless and immune to what is going on which perpetuates the cycle even further. If we can get some social workers and psychologists to counsel the youth, some lawyers to educate the youth to what can happen to them legally, some survivors to tell them that there is another way and to educate them as to the path to taking the other way, and last but not least some youth to actually tell us what is going on and why instead of a panel of adults whom are not linked to the violence maybe we can decrease the violence in our city and save some lives.

What we will be doing is creating a platform to decrease the violence in Chicago by collecting letters, calls, and interviews from both the victims and the perpetrators of violence in our city in this day and time. We will also be collecting information from the youth trapped in this violence as well as stories from survivors of such violence and those imprisoned due to being a part of Chicago's cycle of violence. We will get on as many television talk shows, radio, and news report panels as possible to answer and try to counsel some of those stuck in this violence whether they are the victims or the perpetrators. After the cameras are off we will continue to volunteer time and direction to this cause for a lifetime and pass the cause down to the youth.

Why You Are Being Called

Congratulations! You have made it. You went from Chicago public or private school, came from a low-income home, maybe grew up in a single parent household or have had separated parents, and many other odds. Yet, you have gone to College, completed your degree, and landed that oh so rewarding job. You are either working on a family or preparing to. You have bought property or are planning on it and you are going to do it right here in the city that you came from- Chicago! But wait! Where are you going to move? The crime is too high in this city to move where you came from. You watch the news to the sadness of Chicago's Jennifer Hudson as she deals with what happened with her family. You hear the news of Chicago celebrity R. Kelly's nephew as a victim of violence. But those are celebrities and our hearts go out to them because we have all realized that they are people just like us and like us suffer from a cycle of violence that has loomed over our city long before we came into being. We watch this violence on the news and see it in the streets and are scared to address it let alone speak to it! Well, I want us to speak to violence!!! Violence is tired of being ignored! Violence is tired of you turning the other cheek until it hits home and afterwards doing nothing about it! Violence is spreading because it is a disease being untreated! Let's stop ignoring it and treat it in hopes that it will decrease in our communities.

You will see forums on television on how to quell the violence like, the one on Black Entertainment Television (BET) or the Being Black in America Mini series on CNN, but you never see any panel newscaster ask those involved in the middle of the violence why they participate in such activity--the victims and the shooters. American in a Sense was written by an author who has been both victim of violence and executioner of violence as a possible diagnosis to the violence and disenfranchisement that plagues the people of Chicago and even people all over the world. It is the author's idea that this violence stems from the lack of the natural resources of an area to all people. The reason that we shot at each other and still do is over the limited resources that are readily available to our mindset. It doesn't have to be equal in our day and age, but there needs to be more! We live in a society where a woman can die and leave millions to a family pet-- millions that can aid entire families. This is a society where some make enough to support families for four life times.

The author wants readers to know that he is aware that many of the wealthy give valiantly and he is not looking at the wealthy as the resolution to our problems but their help & resources are needed in order to build the great America as it is truly designed. The author is not looking at the middle class as the solution, not the government, but us all. We all are the American fraternity and it is high time that we act like it! I am my American brothers' and sisters' keeper--are you?

This book is based on the true story of the life of the author. Other information on the different characters involved is based on the lives of the most powerful leaders of organizations throughout the history of Chicago and America. Right now, as the author lives, he has received college degrees in Secondary Education, Liberal Studies, and is within 3 courses of a degree in Educational Leadership and Legal Aspects of Education. The author works for one of the most notable community organizing groups in the City of Chicago I which he places teacher in low-income neighborhoods for the North Lawndale community under a State of Illinois grant. He has worked as a Human Services Specialist, possesses over ten years of training in community outreach in Chicago, and is a father. He wants to aid the successes of your future America but is not allowed. So again what is out there to help him right now? The drug game? Crime? The author doesn't want to see his children suffer; he wants to help his mother and the rest of his family to get to better standards. Part two is coming soon. Here is a reward for reading my book--my gift to you.

The Gift: Sneak peek into Part Two

In an unmarked car in downtown Chicago, Mondo watches with great malice as Michael walks out of the federal building. Thinking to himself, *I know he is going to be the leader one day*, Mondo plots a plan to stop him.

The F.B.I & the youth of Chicago's Street organizations will mark Law for death in a great struggle for restructuring.

Dick was picked up by his staff in a City SUV and taken to his home, with all charges dropped. Dick will fight with Law, the F.B.I, & all forces around to restructure the city. *Its all or nothing in his city.*

Mr. G walked out of the door, lit his cigar and got into his stretch Navigator with his associates. No charges were pressed and a complaint was put in against the FBI for harassment. He has a meeting in a Freemasons lodge scheduled.

Merv and Flaco had a date with a man named Ritty, who had just been promoted in the drug and weapons world of Chicago. A great war ensues on the City's streets as law officers are killed along with even more youth.

Khan would begin a special unit of hand picked agents to investigate the Freemasons as a lead to this organization of assassins that the District Chief spoke about as well as the dealings of the tactical police teams throughout Chicago. Guess who was his main target?

Ritty was in need of a new assistant since Big K was dead and Sweets went off to jail. There is a kid with great potential; here comes Lil Maniak…

- *The Game won't change it will get more fierce.* – HBO's the Wire

OTHER WORKS BY NAS PUBLISHING

COMING THIS EASTER SEASON 2009

Can You Keep a Secret (A Double Novel)

Can you keep a secret? Thousands of years ago all the nations of the civilized world enjoyed peace under one world order until a coalition of secret orders placed a trap to enslave the minds of the people into the Holy books of what became the world's three Major religions. A High Priestess along with twelve members of an Alliance within that coalition had also placed the key to unlocking the trap to all three religions in one of the books entitled the Holy Bible. Hidden in the stories of women in the Bible the key was discovered and removed by the elder men of the society. Open this book and become privy to secret ritual and information that will capture your deepest thoughts.

Open this book a read the secret version of the story of Easter and Christmas in which Mary & Joseph are warrior Priests whom fight with their very lives to protect the future of the rest of humanity. Open this novel and begin the process of true freedom through eliminating the slavery that has your mind anchored in upholding biased gender roles, class, and racism.

www.ingramcontent.com/pod-product-compliance
Lightning Source LLC
Chambersburg PA
CBHW060106260626
47160CB00005B/1821

* 9 7 8 0 6 1 5 2 6 6 4 7 3 *